Halo by the (

By Adam McNelis

To

Big Dandy Andy

Thanks for your support.

All the best mate.

Power on!

Adam

Introduction

It was around 2007, that I first started writing what would become, "Halo by the Oak Tree." I had three key narrative beats in my head that I would write, forget about, re-write, forget about again, and repeat...

After many years of hoarding note pads, with the same scenarios written over and over again, in 2013 I eventually found the inspiration to stop just re-writing the broad strokes and concentrate on putting it all together into one cohesive narrative. This came about when, having purchased a weekend ticket, I went to the Glasgow Comic Con for the first time, which then took place at the CCA (Centre for Contemporary Arts) in Sauchiehall Street.

It was a real lightening bolt moment, and although I wasn't looking to write or draw a comic or graphic novel (yet), just being there with so many happy, interesting, and creative people, it gave me this charge; this real buzz and desire to do something creative. Having spent most of my Saturday there, I immediately went to a shop and bought a pen and a pad, before settling down to a window seat in the iCafe across the road from the CCA. There, I sought to start writing something that would incorporate all three sections that

I had been repeatedly writing over the years. I wanted to join it all together.

A couple of nights a week, I would drive to the iCafe to write, my new writing venue of choice, and in between creative quandaries I would watch the world go by in the form of the hustle and bustle of Sauchiehall Street. As I write this, Sauchiehall Street has had a terrible time of late, but it will return, and when it does it will be better and more vibrant than ever.

As time passed, there would be other moments that inspired me to keep going; on 22 April 2014, I attended 'An Evening with Mark Millar' at the Glasgow Caledonian University, and hearing what he had to say about his prolific career and creative process, it further fuelled my desire to finish this book, by hook or by crook. Because, as Mark said that night, "an idea can change the world."

But with like most of these things, time would slip through my fingers, and I never needed much encouragement to procrastinate, not to mention, that between then and now I also got married and became a father.

I love podcasts, and it was in listening to the likes of Kevin Smith and Joe Rogan, and their respective network of friends, that I gained a better mental outlook; in that every time I asked myself "why would I want to do this?" I would change it to "why would I *not* want to do this?"

Listening to the podcasts, combined with practicing Transcendental Meditation, it gave me the inner confidence and determination to see this through, regardless if only four people and their dog ever read it.

Some of this book is semi-autobiographical, although most of it isn't. The characters are not based on any real individuals; they are a combination of various people I have met, and my trusty imagination.

The opinions expressed in this book that touch upon subjects, such as; family, faith, sex, gender roles, self-esteem, golf, bald people, mental health, middle-aged dog walkers, and so on, also differ greatly from my own, for the most part.

Socially, I have always been a story teller, which is a blessing and a curse; I have seen many a person's eyes roll, followed by "hurry up and get to the point." This book gave me the opportunity to explore and wrestle with ideas, conjure moments that made me laugh, and some that made me cry, cast away some old ghosts, and most importantly, reaffirm my belief that no matter what comes your way, you can deal with it.

"Halo by the Oak Tree" took longer to finish than it should have done, and maybe as long as it needed to be. If you are one of the four people, or you are the dog, who has decided to read this, thank you! I hope you enjoy it.

Power on,

Adam McNelis (November 2018)

@MrAdamMcNelis

….that's M C N E L I S   (kisses)

Dedication

For my love, "Miss Lady"

A & D

CHAPTER 1

I have this reoccurring dream that I can fly, and no one seems to care. The fact that no one acknowledges the sheer awesomeness of my winged majesty provides me with a real sense of injustice that I carry with me throughout my dream state. I mean, I don't show off with it – I am not doing anything crazy or irresponsible; like interfering with the flight paths of planes, or whooshing around the sky pretending that I am some kind of super hero or anything like that. All of my flying related activities consists of random stuff; like landing on top of bus stops, just to take in new perspectives, before nipping off to the shops, and when I get home I fly in through the living room window instead of using the front door, you know, because I can. I think that probably the cheekiest thing that I have done in all of my flying about, is a couple of times I have swooped down and stolen some chips off of a random passer-by, just one or two, nothing too greedy. Often, I will sit on top of lamp posts and just watch the world go by. All the while, no one on the street meets my gaze, my suspicion is that people see me buzzing and swooping about the place and think, "look at him, showing off with that stupid bastarding flying malarkey." But it's not like that, I can fly, so I am flying – I'm not trying to one-up the non-flying masses. I am sure that if I couldn't fly, and I saw someone else who could, I'd be impressed, interested, happy for them. But not for me – you could say, if you were into puns, that no one seems to give a flying fuck.

Most mornings, I wake up from my dream and I think, "what the hell is wrong with me? I need to get a grip of all of this persecution-complex, self-pitying shit." Dreams haven't had this much baring on my life since my primary school days when I used to have a reoccurring anxiety dream that I was running about the corridors, bare arsed, with my nudge hanging out. To be fair, my head's been moosh for well over a year now, I guess my crazy dreams are just a bit of light relief from all the over-thinking that I have been doing, trying to make sense of everything that went on. Now, having had more than enough time alone with my thoughts, I have come to the conclusion – it's all about experience and context.

You see, in my near twenty years on this Earth I've never known hunger, poverty, racism, or any other kind of abuse; whether it be mental, physical, or sexual. I have never been faced with the grief of losing a loved one, or any other potential human horror for that matter. So having never really had to deal with adversity, I find myself in this weird state of limbo, in that I know, logically, I should take a step back, put everything in its place, and move forward into adulthood, and try to transform into some semblance of a real life person. But I can't do that, oh no, I've been way too busy feeling sorry for myself. Yes, I have thrown myself the most epic of pity parties, and I am only now, after eighteen months, anywhere near to getting my head firmly out of my arse and giving myself the royal slap around the dish that I know I need.

It all started with the band. All my life I had played it safe, then the one time that I tried, I mean *really* tried, that I truly cared about anything, that I ever really put my balls out there and said, "check out these big smelly bad bastards", it all came crashing down. When the dust settled, I looked around and all I had was my newly found status as a loner, a shit-ton of credit-card debt, and for the lack of a better description, a broken heart.

Until the band, I had never really applied myself to anything, ever. A trait I now put down to a childhood spent avoiding competitive sports; at the first sign of resistance or a challenge, I would walk away. The band was a vehicle, it manoeuvred me through uncharted social territory to lands of new-found confidence, excitement, and girls. The only local girl to show any interest in me, before the band, goes to another school. It's not nice to say, but the word is that she is an absolute unashamed dong addict, and again, not proud of it, she is a funny shape and she looks like an absolute riot; her nickname is "Jabba the House", for fucks sake.

There's this little voice inside my head, I hear it every day, it says, "shut up you pussy." When I think about what happened, there it is, that voice, diminishing any entitlement I have to my sense of hurt and lingering aftertaste of betrayal. Ultimately, it serves to highlight what a fool I've been. In all the thinking, all the mulling over, all the contemplation, all I really know for certain is – I have never been so royally bummed out, and it's all my fault. In this first true test of character, I have shown myself up to be sorely lacking, I have been such an absolute dumpling.

There were four of us; Scott on vocals, Donald on bass, "Trumpet" on drums, and I played lead guitar. When I think about the whole thing, it's like a frenetic cinematic montage in my mind. It just built and built, it was better than I could have imagined, four best pals without a care in the world, having the time of our lives, just jamming and laughing. It was the most laughter I had ever known.

I started playing when I was about fourteen years old after I found an old beaten-up acoustic guitar in our loft. I was completely mesmerised when my Dad said that it was his and that he used to play it back when he was a young buck. I had never seen, or heard of, him playing it, but all credit to him, he showed me the basic chords and I just seemed to get the knack of it. I would take the bus up to Glasgow and hang around a few of the guitar shops, pestering the sales guys for a shot of the guitars and picking up hints and tips whenever I could. From there, I started listening to all kinds of music from about the 1950s onwards, I wanted to have an appreciation and understanding of what popular music was all about throughout the decades.

I had been playing for about a year and I still hadn't told my friends, I guess I thought that they would slag me off about it; the general perception was that the folk who hung around the Music Department were dusty fuckwits with strange politicians' haircuts, teachers' pets, and total zephs. Then, one by one, my friends and I realised that coincidentally we had all been playing an instrument – on the sneak, and like that, we were out of the musical closet.

Scott didn't need to join a band or anything like that to pull girls, they flocked to him, he just had it; that tractor-beam aura, such effortless skills. But what a singer, his voice would never waver, never crack under pressure, plus he had such great range. Having him on vocals was like having a panther for a front man; cool, smooth, and with real presence. Christ, it sounds like I want to give him a good riding myself, but there was just no denying, simply put – he was shit hot. He could play the guitar too, but for whatever reason he wasn't really interested in playing it as part of the band. He never really sought to learn anything fancier than the basic chords, but when you're mojo personified and as good with the girls as he was, he didn't have to. Donald used to play the bass like a lead guitar, it was incredible. For a wee white guy from Paisley he had a serious well of funk in his soul. Then there was Trumpet. Trumpet's real name was Crawford, a name he absolutely detested, he used to say that it was "poofy" and that he resented his parents for calling him it. Randomly, somebody once commented that, so contorted was his face when in the throes of smashing his drums, that it made his face look like a trumpet, and as bizarre as it sounds, he liked it, so the name stuck and he was never called Crawford by any of us ever again. It is a bit of a band cliché to say that drummers are always mad, but in Trumpet's case it was definitely true, the guy was completely off his tits, a real character, a loveable oddity. You would try and have a normal interaction with him, and instantly, he would do or say something that left you laughing or feeling completely alienated. A walking fucking case study.

We began jamming in our school's Music Department and instantly it just clicked. We used to do a cover of the song, "Peace Frog" by the Doors, that we would play over and over again until it was completely polished. Then one day we decided to give it a proper go and write our own songs. During the initial period of the band, I felt as though I had contributed, but no more than that. It wasn't until I put forward some songs that I had written for consideration, that much to my surprise, the guys absolutely loved. From there, I went from a mere contributor, to a driving force. At first I thought that perhaps the boys were just being polite, but it soon became clear that their support was genuine, a collective sentiment that I grew to crave like a drug. To my continued surprise, and delight, the boys just seemed to keep lapping up my ideas, and for the first time in my life I felt this real surge of confidence, not just putting-a-brave-face-on-it bullshit. I felt like I had the skills and the juice to create something, hone it, nurture it, and really take it somewhere.

First we had to come up with a name for the band, I considered calling us Dog Shit Delicious as it is a bit of an attention grabber. However, we wouldn't be able to perform in many places with a name like that, and we really didn't want people to think that not only did we eat dog shit, but that we also thought it was tasty. I wanted us to sound cool, slick, exotic, but also not taking ourselves too seriously. Then it came to me, and our band had its name, we were The Midnite Stealth Assassins. I suggested "midnite" instead of "midnight" so that people who didn't know us would presume we were foreign, and ultimately a bit more interesting than four local baw-bags. I wanted people to hear our name, or see it on a poster, and think, "that band *must* be cool."

We had to get a look, and although we weren't entirely sure what we would settle on, we knew that we had to look sharp, we couldn't be four ordinary dressed gonks; in our school uniforms, up on stage with our slouched shoulders and spotty faces. So we established some ground rules, and it started with – no trainers. Other bands may have been and gone, who got away with wearing gutties, but not us. No daft t-shirts either, you can't be up on stage looking like you're on a holiday that you won on the back of a cereal box. It was agreed, that we would keep it to smart/casual, preferably darker clothes, to set the tone, and evolve from there. The overall sentiment was, "be cool – but never be too cool."

The sound we agreed on for the band was basically dance music masked as rock music. We wanted plenty of bass and drums, in the hope that people would want to dance and jump around to us – sprinkle Scott's vocals on top and you would have music that people will want to pump to. We also agreed that we wanted to create an allure about us and what we were up to, to grow a word-of-mouth PR bonanza, to get people hooked and hungry for more. I wanted the stars, and I wanted everyone to know.

We would rehearse, then rehearse, then rehearse some more. We had a real chemistry, it was all so effortless. Donald or I would bring a riff or a chord pattern to the table for consideration, we would then incorporate it into some kind of structure, then I would put words to it, and once I was happy with that, Scott would lay his vocals down. That was the system and it seemed to work, each of us comfortable with our own roles within the band, and with what each member was contributing. There's no denying, far more of what I put forward was implemented than was rejected. I loved the spark of it all, and I think that the boys were happy to see me with a bit of gallusness about me, as opposed to hiding in the shadows or skulking around like a floppy cock, like I usually did. With each practice session, both as a band and as a bunch of friends, we got tighter and tighter. It felt as though we were really on to something, then it got to a point where we said, "we're ready, let's get a gig."

There was this electricity in the air, it was like, "yeah man, let's do this, let's fucking do this!"

Our first performance was at the school talent show. Anyone who knew us probably had us pigeon-holed as a group of school corridor drifters, unlikely to be partaking in any kind of public performance, and for the rest who didn't know us, they simply didn't care. Although, backstage there was a snidey, condescending, arsey vibe being aimed our way from all of the Fifth and Sixth years. As we were the only Fourth year band present, the other bands were older and all knew each other. We were an unknown quantity, but not for long. As we approached the stage we were as relaxed as could be, we knew that we had put in the hours, we had done the work. We got called up on stage, some people sniggered when our band's name was read out, but we soon wiped the smile off their faces. Trumpet counted us in, "one, a two, a one, two, three, four", then whooft – Trumpet's drums kicked in, then together Donald's bass and my lead guitar. Then out of the shadows at the side of the stage, like a big handsome bastard vampire, Scott slowly eased into centre-stage, took the mic from its stand, and in those next few minutes, we melted the face off of every last mother fucker in there with relentless waves of epic audio shaggery. When it was time for my guitar solo, Trumpet gave Donald the nod, who in turn gave me the nod, to give it laldy and stretch the solo out for as long as I wanted. In that moment, I felt like a God. The four of us were synchronicity personified, our audience, made up of fellow pupils and members of the faculty, were completely and utterly blown away. The song built up and up and up, and right at the perfect spot, we hit our crescendo. Trumpet fizzled out the drums and with one final strum of the guitars, we were done.

For a micro second there was silence, before an almighty roar consumed the entire gym hall. The crowd went wild, it was insane; clapping, cheering, smiling, and waving. We stood there for a moment, just to soak it all in. We all looked at each other – holy shit, we're on to something here. We walked backstage, even some of the other bands were coming up and congratulating us, others were shaking their heads in disbelief and asking us, "who are you guys?", and quietly amongst themselves you heard them ask each other, "did you have any idea?"

The ripple effect in the socialsphere was instant; random people were saying hello to us in the corridors and girls were making enquiries about us. This was all new, and very much welcome, territory. From nowhere, we started to get a lot of invites to house parties, something that never used to happen, but we were determined to keep our focus on rehearsing. Plus, it gave us that little bit of mystique that we had been looking for, that if despite the most popular people asking us to pop by for a beer, we were unavailable.

From that point nothing else mattered, for me anyway. A couple of the boys mentioned in passing that they wanted to gain some decent qualifications, I presume as a safety net should things not pan out, but I firmly believed that it was all or nothing. I kept writing – creatively, I felt in the zone, and by now we had fifteen or so songs that we considered solid. I really believed in what we were doing, I started to think about which of our songs would go onto our debut album, which tracks would be our singles, and which would be our B-Sides. Unknown to us at the time, someone in the audience had filmed our school performance on a camcorder, and although the video quality was pretty poor, the sound quality was surprisingly good. Donald knew a tech wizard who was able to get the footage of our performance online, and as a direct result of someone seeing our performance via the internet, we got to play a local community carnival. Now folk out-with our school were starting to discover us.

For me it was simple; just keep pushing, that's all we had to do, and the possibilities would be boundless. I just had to be patient, a couple of the guys mentioned that they didn't want to leave school until after Sixth year. At first that really frustrated me, two years is a long time, but then I realised that we could practice every day, and I wouldn't have my parents asking me about going to university or getting a full time job. Although, I did need some money, so I got a job flipping burgers. I came up with a whole host of made-up reasons as to why I could not work past 7pm at weekends as to not affect my ability to play gigs, and the job provided me with enough pocket money to eek by.

The months flew past, I told a few of the familiar faces that I had gotten to know in the guitar shops, who were all deeply wired into the Glasgow music scene, about our growing reputation with each new gig that we performed, and how we had now managed to get a few videos online, and that we were starting to generate a bit of buzz. By this point, we had been together as a band for two years, and school was almost over – this was not the time to be shy, it was the time to unzip our chompers and wave them about the place. One of the guys was called Roy, he was a senior member of staff at the esteemed, Chief's Guitars shop, and although the rumour was that he had played session guitar for some big international acts in the 1980s, he was known for keeping his cards close to his chest, not one for flaunting his fifteen minutes of fame. One day during an otherwise unremarkable bit of chit-chat, Roy asks me to direct him to our videos online so that, if he "got around to it", he could check them out.

I would pop into Chief's Guitars every now and then, hoping desperately that Roy would approach me and tell me what he thought about our videos online, had he watched them. But every time I would go in Roy was either with someone or in the stock room. As much as I wanted to be pushy, I knew that I couldn't be that way with Roy, he was old school. Then, when I had been in so many times that I had almost forgotten about Roy, I bumped into him, and he immediately asked me what age I was. I told him that I had just turned eighteen and he seemed happy about that. Although, his tone quickly shifted when he asked me who the youngest in the band was. When I told him that it was Donald he very impatiently snapped back at me, "and when the fuck is he eighteen?" I hastily replied, "not for another three weeks. Why?" To my complete astonishment, Roy instantly chilled out again and then proceeded to tell me, as if it were nothing at all, that he has us a spot at King Tut's Wah Wah Hut in six weeks, if we want it. If we want it? Of course we fucking wanted it! Even strange cats that aren't into music have heard of King Tut's Wah Wah Hut. It is a hallowed place, synonymous with providing new talent with the opportunity to shine. It has been host to some of the biggest bands, not only from Scotland or the UK, but from around the world; Radiohead, Crowded House, The Verve, Blur, Coldplay, Beck, Manic Street Preachers, Teenage Fanclub, and Primal Scream. Oasis were signed by Creation Records after playing there, and they did no bad.

We were told that the venue guys wanted to make sure that we were all at least eighteen years old, as they didn't want the arse-ache of having to worry about under-age piss heads. After all, they had a business to run and they knew there was a good chance that a lot of our fan-base would be borderline in terms of being legally allowed to drink. If the band was of age then the bouncers checking peoples' I.D would take care of the rest. We were allocated a slot whereby we could fit in around eight songs, but we were warned that if we were gash, or things just weren't going our way, we could get the chop at any time. We had to be on the ball.

I told the guys and they were thrilled, mostly. A couple of them muttered something about their exams coming up, or some pish like that, but there was only one thing on my mind, *the* gig – it would be the culmination of two years' worth of hard work, the pinnacle of our high school experience, symbolising our ascendency towards new and exciting heights. We had six weeks, six weeks to make sure that we had a set locked down and that we looked the part. When it came to our instruments, this whole time we had been playing the same old rickety shit pieces. It was time for an upgrade – to be somebodies, we had to look like somebodies. I decided that it was time to "speculate to accumulate", a phrase that I had heard one of the managers say on Match of the Day. I applied for two credit cards, and they were approved. I would surely have both paid off in no time at all, it was fate that this gig would send us on an upward trajectory to global rock stardom, I had no doubt in my mind.

Exam Leave commences, and with all of this free time on our hands, I start to pester the boys morning, noon, and night about getting us together to rehearse. This time there was less muttering and more flat-out moaning from the boys, but nothing major, nothing I couldn't handle. The mission was clear; get so polished musically, that in no time at all, the only thing we'd then have to worry about polishing was our Gold and Platinum discs, hung proudly above the Jacuzzis in our respective mansions.

Gig night, and for the first time I was nervous. So much so, that I even had to go and take a shit at the venue, and I rarely shit anywhere other than home. But this wasn't the time to over analyse my turd-action pattern, I had taken the lead in all of this, I had to clean my arse and clear my head, wash my hands, and get my game face on. I got myself sorted quickly and re-joined my bandmates. In the dressing room, no one was really talking to each other, we knew what we had to do, so there was no point gibbering about it. We met in an impromptu huddle, the battle cry had always been, "let's do this", so once more we let it out, and just then we heard, "please welcome to the stage, The Midnite Stealth Assassins!"

We get on stage, adrenaline pumping, the few faces I can see are a blur, the rest of the crowd is shrouded in darkness as all of the lights are on us. But despite my earlier pre-gig jitters, I feel more comfortable than ever. I think to myself, "the crowd are on our side, so let's keep it that way."

We fly straight into it, as in, I mean we really get stuck in; get completely lost in all of the sound and the lights, the sweat and the fury. The whole time I am giggling to myself and thinking, "surely one of us is going to balls it up here", but no, each song goes exactly how we rehearsed it, and is met by rapturous applause. I keep waiting for a dud reaction, but it never comes.

And like that, the gig was over. It had gone by in a flash. All I can really remember clearly at the end was that we got a really good cheer when Scott belted out his final words to the audience, "thank you, good night", and that we were completely drenched in our own sweat. I was proud, proud of the guys, proud of myself too, it felt as though we had written the perfect first chapter in what would be a long and illustrious story.

We make our way backstage and I am expecting us all to be jumping around the place and completely hyper, in a prolonged state of ecstasy with having being able to pull off our first really big gig – plus, in terms of performance, it was damn near perfection. But no, to my complete astonishment, the guys start to pack away their gear and make locker room small talk about the gig like they've just played a game of five-a-side football. I was expecting battle cries, sweaty celebratory man-hugs, and declarations of victory inspired debauchery. The overwhelming sense of anti-climax catches me completely off-guard, my brain simply cannot compute the even keeled, mild, dinner at your Granny's like atmosphere among the guys. One of them starts talking about his exams, I cannot help but think, "is this twonk for real?" Did Led Zeppelin sit about like this after a gig, like they were having tea and crumpets? I don't fucking think so. They were most probably up to all kinds of depraved dark shit that I could not fully fathom.

Trumpet's uncle had done us a solid and offered to deliver and collect the equipment. Two hours after the gig we are in a bar on St. Vincent Street and I am still trying to piece this mad night together; they aren't even talking about the gig, at all, anymore. Scott told us that he had to head to Firewater on Sauchiehall Street as he was meeting a sort in there, so we decided to tag along. I say "we", but I had no input, still in a state of shock, I merely followed the guys around like I was a lobotomised Yorkshire Terrier.

As soon as we arrive in Firewater, we start buying rounds of beers. I have never really been able to handle alcohol, but given how this night has panned out I can't help but think, "bollocks to it, why not?" As the night goes on, I continue to barely say a word, I position myself close to a speaker so that I can use the excuse of not being able to hear anything as the reason to duck out of small talk. The lights come on and it's time to go home, but not before we follow the time-honoured tradition of going for a kebab before trying to flag down a taxi.

Walking a couple of steps behind the boys, in my drunken haze, it dawns on me that despite it being the first time in my life that I had been sure about something, so sure, I had gone too far, too deep, and a little bit mental. I had been humbled completely as the result of my tunnel vision - ignoring the harsh facts, denying the reality, that what was my everything, was simply a hobby to my friends. Without consultation, so sure of our collective dreams and destiny, I powered on and maxed out two credit cards to the tune of £7,000+ on equipment for the band. Full of piss and vinegar, I decided to tell my pals this little monetary factoid. Their reaction – it was like an intervention, like they have for alcoholics, drug addicts, and frenzied wank enthusiasts.

What followed hit me like a tsunami of truth, the sheer weight of the reality-check was almost too much to handle. It was jovial initially, which I presume was out of shock, but they soon became uncharacteristically serious, telling me that they thought I must have lost my mind, that I had been completely reckless and irresponsible, and that... they all had their own plans, plans that had nothing to do with the band.

They were probably right. Who am I kidding? They were right! But why, why did they have to tell me when I was drunk? I walk about most days thinking that I am a decent enough wee guy, but every now and then when I drink, alcohol seems to have this ruthless knack of stripping me bare to the point where it unveils this fragile, whimpering, insecure, angry, and often venomous, little shitehawk. As the boys just stood there looking at me, having got what they had to say off of their chests, the magnitude of what they had just told me; that they were not on board with sacrificing everything for the band, and that they wanted to carve out their lives in their own separate ways, it was simply too much.

I had interwoven my ego, my purpose for being, my dreams and aspirations, into our band, to abandon the band now was to blow me out the airlock and cast me out into deep space. I could feel the anger rising from the tips of my toes, up my legs, through my torso, bypassing my fists, and by the time it reached my lips it was pure unfiltered poison. No one was spared from my volley of verbal diarrhoea, so much so, that to my eternal shame I recall saying, "and you, you acne ridden jug-eared cunt" to Donald, who has neither acne nor jug ears, and is quite possibly one of the nicest human beings I have ever met. But this was just one example of the many vicious verbal atom bombs I dropped that fateful night. We got our hands on each other, we had rarely even argued before, and then for a moment it looked as though the boys were about to collectively "slap me good looking." But after a bit of a tussle, they let me go. As they walked away, they shouted things like, "tosser", "prick", and "fucking idiot", and the more I have thought about it, I can't really argue with them.

Shortly after, it felt like time had stopped, I was completely numb. I felt truly betrayed; we were meant to be in this together and just like that, they dropped the whole thing. When all was said and done, I looked, and felt, like a massive tit. The harsh truth is that I needed those guys, I could never go it alone, I had been so sure that we were in it together. The magnitude of how deeply it affected me caused me to "check out" in every sense. I used to be a nervous natterer, now I am painfully quiet, and, the sad thing is, I can't be sure if anyone has even noticed. Licking my wounds this whole time, doing nothing but mull over it again and again, I think I am ready to at least try and get my life back on track. But where do I start?

CHAPTER 2

My arse isn't "screen ready." For example; Mel Gibson's arse, at the start of "Lethal Weapon", when he gets out of bed and takes a beer from the fridge, that is a presentable arse. Mine? I would be self-conscious about sleeping with a girl when my arse is in its current predicament; as although I don't have much stubble on my face or hair on my chest, my legs and arse are a hairy fiasco. If a girl was to glide her hand across my butt cheeks right now, all sorts of madness is possible; she could get carpet burn on her palm, or her fingers would get shish kebabbed with generous helpings of toilet paper balls and stink nuggets. It is matters such as these that I need to address; "eat the elephant, one bite at a time"; shave that ass, introduce it to a dedicated moisturising plan, do some squats. The mind boggles, the mind wanders.

I have been feeling very lonely for quite some time now. The longer it goes on, as I become more and more isolated and, ultimately, more introspective, it is as though I have contracted some kind of social leprosy, and the more I try to shake it off, the worse it seems to get.

I go so long without any interaction with real life people, that when an opportunity does arise, it feels almost predetermined that I will fail; stiff, awkward, lacking the day-to-day practice that would provide the social lubrication to enable me to engage with others with any real sense of flow, purpose, or spark.

I appear to have become hard-wired with the presumption and, more worryingly, the acceptance, that probably no one would ever bother their (well groomed) arse with me, and why should they? When someone does engage me in conversation of any kind, I come across as jarring and generally, a little bit *off* – basically, the village space cadet. It's all on me, until I banish this sad-sack "poor me" shite, I know that it does not make me an attractive proposition for company and fun times.

Maybe, with all these negative thoughts swirling around my noggin, I should just shut up, man up, fuck up, get over myself, and get a grip? The best way that I can describe loneliness, in my experience, is that it gets in you, on you, it hurts your heart and skews your thoughts, and no matter how much you wrestle with it, it feels as though you may as well be wearing a massive neon sign, that simply reads, "stay away. I am a nob head." At least if I had a nob for a head, it would be a bit of a conversation starter.

I hope that I can straighten all of this out sooner rather than later. I just need to chill – as I have heard people say in the past, that you are more likely to fall in love when you are not looking for it, so maybe it could be the same for me when it comes to making friends and banishing all of my mad shite – relax, and it will all be parties, cold beers, and blowjobs from here on in.

However, I'm finding it hard to realign my thoughts; to think clearer and more positively. For example; six months ago, some information fell onto my lap, information that I could have done without. Donald's Mum bumped into my Mum in the supermarket, and completely oblivious to the awful shitting anguish that this would cause me, my Mum then subsequently proceeded to relay the entire catalogue of intel that she had gathered – that Donald and Trumpet had both completed their first year at Glasgow University, Scott was working at his Dad's large construction firm, and that the three of them were just about to go travelling around the world together as part of an early gap-year. My Mum didn't know any better, all she knew was that we had had a falling out "of sorts", but she has no idea of just how pickled my head is right now; being without them, missing out on their new adventures and stories. Regardless, how I wish she had forgotten to fill me in, about any of it.

I didn't have a chance of getting into university straight from school; I had put all of my eggs in one basket and downed tools academically the moment that the band started cookin'. In terms of an apprenticeship or anything like that, I am terrible with numbers, I can barely count my fingers, and somehow everything seems to require maths in some form or another. Besides, I wasn't in any position to buy into the short-term pain and long-term gain of an apprenticeship, I had my credit card debt to pay off.

I managed to get a job in a call centre, taking insurance claims. The job title is First Contact Agent – I find it undeniably dreadful and completely soul destroying. But despite my lack of job satisfaction, and my perpetual state of borderline sedation, I seem to have the knack of being able to just rattle on through it and, according to my Monthly Manager Reviews, I am apparently quite good at it. Here was me thinking that I was going to be a Rock God, playing stadium tours, and frequently orchestrating squadrons of lingerie models around my schmeckle. Oh well.

I spend my days talking to people from all over the UK, and such is the diverse range of accents on this island that we share, I have really had to develop my ear for it. I have to be able to understand what people are saying and record their claims as accurately, and as quickly, as possible. One second I can be talking to a crofter from Thurso about "the weather up there", the next, I am being slagged about the state of Scottish football by some right "proppa geeza" from "Laandan". We get them all; Brummies, Scousers, Mancs, Bristolians, and so on. And in turn, I need to robotify my West of Scotland accent to make myself understood also. In real life, I hardly ever swear or talk about sex, and luckily for me, when I am in work, I am able to avoid doing both completely, but inside my head – my mind is awash with foul language, dirty thoughts, and fairly frequent bouts of simmering rage.

The pay is dreadful, and the layout and overall energy of the working environment is akin to some bleak dystopian future, but it does have one perk – Katie's bum. It is just a lovely wee unit – I'd really like to cup it, pat it, spank it, and gnaw on it, and in no particular order. I find it fascinating, how the horn can be so distracting, so potent in clouding the brain completely; walking about like a starved, deprived beast with no peace of any kind, not until one's own piece is "dealt with". Maybe, as a species, we would get far more done if we weren't so ill in the breeks.

When I was young, I loved drawing, playing with my action figures, and making dens with my friends. Then one day my balls dropped, and it was as if I had been laser-zapped by aliens, leaving me instantly possessed by an all-conquering, mind-controlling force.

All the tropes of childhood gone in a flash, and now I was just another young fool inducted into the league of horny creature slaves. However, since things went pear-shaped with my friends and my social life completely evaporated, overall, I have been slightly dormant in that department. I still wake up most mornings to a trusty storky, and skelp it about from time to time, but sometimes it just seems futile. Often, I lie in the bath and my floating flaccid nob stares back at me, and I think, "you disappoint me son. You should be out doing all sorts. Plus, tidy these pubes up, they're a disgrace." But I don't, I just carry on with my 1970s-style, non-sheered, fro-pwabs. So, it is not just my wild arse that needs addressed, I need to get serious about my pubic maintenance also. I will need to buy a large industrial tarpaulin at this rate; post grooming, it will look like I have just shaved a bear.

I have heard people say that yanking your plank is "practice for the big game", but to continue that analogy further, my big game fixture schedule is well and truly clear at present, not even a bounce game on the horizon. With actual women? Please, the little mojo I had previously is well and truly goosed.

But it wasn't always like this – despite the girls being more likely to want to eat their own face than kiss me during my first few years at high school, Jabba the House excluded, when I was fourteen, I lost my virginity to girl called Samantha. Samantha didn't go to my school, she was the niece of a woman who lived a few doors down from us. Samantha came to stay with her aunty for a long weekend, her aunty asked if I would play with her. Against all of the odds, and my wildest expectations, having only met her a couple of hours, just sitting around my room, Samantha grabbed me by my little salty snail, threw me down, jumped on me, and instructed me to let her know when I was at the "tickly bit", so that she could jump off just in time. For three days in a row, we engaged in multiple short jaunts of fumbling shaggery, with not one of these special moments lasting more than about three minutes, each time playing Russian roulette with the reckless horn-fuelled lunacy that is, "the withdraw method." I was like a little human automatic garden hose, just spinning about, firing my magic beans all over the fucking place, just anywhere but in her burger.

A couple of times after a quick poomp, Samantha would lie on my bed, her backside facing me, and for a laugh, I would sit up and start to play the bongos on her bum-cheeks. I would only do it for a few seconds, and Samantha used to giggle about it, such was the silly nonsense of it all. I suspect that there is no truer indicator that your sexual partner really likes you, than when they happily let you play the bongos on their bum-cheeks, post-coitus.

And like that, she was gone. I have never seen, or heard of her, since – a sex angel who came to steal my cherry, before vanishing out of my life as quickly as she had entered it. I don't think I even told my friends about her, or how she opened my eyes to such lovely possibilities – I doubt that my friends would have believed me anyway. Since then, I have not come close to repeating anything remotely similar to what happened, that beautiful bank holiday weekend, when our families thought we were up-stairs playing the SEGA Master System.

Now, it must surely be a positive sign, that maybe I am not dead, knowing that whenever Katie bends down to get her bag, or even just walks past me, I just want her to park on my face and smoosh about. I *really* try to be discreet, but sometimes I probably make it more obvious than I would ideally like. Quick glances are all it is – "my thoughts are my own", I keep reminding myself, and I would genuinely never want to make her feel uncomfortable. But from my perspective, I have to take the positives from this, after all, who would have thought that the mere sight of a tidy bum-bum could signify the thawing of my hibernating libido. It does get me thinking – at school we would receive these classes every so often that were designed, I guess, as an effort to help guide us on our journey into adulthood. One of the things that they emphasised to us, especially the boys, was, "do not objectify the opposite sex" – which also, coincidently, disregarded any possibility that any of the pupils might have the audacity to be anything other than heterosexual. I can understand the motive behind the narrow definition, in terms of framing it in only in heterosexual terms, after all, we were being taught in a Catholic school. However, I still cannot get my head around the idea of objectifying someone as *necessarily* being a bad thing. There are countless paintings, songs, and poems, where artists have dared to bare their soul in expressing their passion for the *object* of their desire. Maybe the people who have a problem with being objectified are looking at things all wrong; that they should perhaps take it as a compliment, lighten up, not over-think it, and move on. As I am not sure that to objectify someone automatically discounts their hopes, dreams, character, scruples, or intelligence. Or maybe I just don't get it, fuck knows really. All I know for sure is that, undeniably, Katie's wee rump walking by, her butt cheeks "eating a penny caramel", is the highlight of my day.

I don't kid myself, not for a second, that Katie would touch me with a bargepole, but as things stand, she hasn't shown any negativity towards me. I don't know what I would do if Katie ever acknowledged my voyeurism, or called me out on it, or went to the next level and reported me. As to me, that would be crazy. I haven't heard any gossip or insinuations that I am considered a creeper, so it is my conclusion that such is the awkwardness that oozes out of every facet of my being, Katie does not see me as any kind of threat – probably, just a bit of a saddo really; as I mope about like a torn bin-bag, or some kind of neutered cousin. I am most likely just another drone colleague to her, I may as well be a fucking fax machine. Or, perhaps I give myself too much credit, there is every chance that she does not notice me, AT ALL.

Besides, Katie keeps her cards close to her chest, even with me doing my best nosey, I don't know that much about her, despite us having worked only a few feet away from each other for over six months. From the bits and bobs I hear in passing, no one seems to know if she is single or not, or what she likes to do at the weekend, and so on.

The only lady in here who shows me the light of day is Joyce. Joyce is a classy older lady; she's funny and friendly and dresses like a hot-shot lawyer from a 90s TV show. If she was thirty years younger I would most certainly eye-beast her from across the office. If I were to guess, I would say that Joyce is in her late 50s, somehow the age gap between us enables me to just relax and talk to her. Joyce and I have a rapport, a nice bit of chemistry, which I have found to be an incredibly rare thing, and what I guess is probably the most important factor in any relationship, platonic or otherwise.

Then there is my Team Leader, Victoria. Victoria is *the* success story in here. Such is her enthusiasm and commitment, that when a senior regional post came up, she applied, and much to an entire team of her bosses' collective fury and jealousy, she got it. She leap-frogged right over the lot of them, and their horrible po-faces. Victoria will be relocating to Head Office in the coming months – somehow, fuck knows how, she became passionate about all this turgid grey insurance sludge and her sheer unbreakable enthusiasm has powered her forward to a great new opportunity.

Victoria seems to like me enough. I think it's because I turn up, log on, grind out, and don't give her any arse-ache. From time to time, I'll even stay on if we are a bit short-staffed because, as almost too horrendously pathetic to dwell on, I rarely have anywhere better to go. All I tend to do is go home and fall asleep in front of the TV, often fully clothed; shoes still on, the lot.

Victoria is alright, I guess, but only in very small doses. I do often wonder though, just how sincere she actually is, I mean, surely no one can smile that much naturally? She is like a laser focused air stewardess on amphetamines; no matter what shit comes her way, that smile of hers stays firmly painted on. Victoria does this thing, that when she smiles, she locks her jaw together, like she has been asked to so by her dentist. And when she smiles, it's never gradually – Victoria pops those smiles like one of those grotesquely exploited child beauty queens. Then there's the wacky skin colour, Victoria needs a "word in her ear" regarding her fake tan. I am trying to be all "to each their own", and I am certainly in no place to judge, and if going for a sunbed is your thing... but Victoria goes way too often, she is a wild funky should-be-brown orangey colour that can only be attributed to some serious form of body dysmorphia. That ubiquitous smile, the bright orange skin, and the sheer intensity that beams out of her, it all freaks me out a bit. Not to mention, her tendency to invade your personal space to the point where you can smell what she ate for breakfast. Overall, my strategy for dealing with Victoria is – I speak when spoken to, and try to get by with minimal interaction.

I want so much to get my life back on track, I don't need Victoria's hurricane of "hiya guuuuuuys" office corporate-wank-speak bullshit up in my zone. Victoria may have done well for herself, but from where I am sitting I can't help but feel sometimes that she has surrendered who she truly is to be a company shill; all front, a human PR machine, a paper-thin orange coloured veneer. I wonder if Victoria would ever deviate from this hologram she's projecting of herself to reveal a glimpse of the real her, and not some pish that she read in some Corporate Communication Mein Kampf. For all my misgivings, I know that in my deepest thoughts in the dead of the night, I fear that I am a fucking husk of a human being, desperately trying to open up a path to a better sense of self, gain some perspective, and ultimately, a semblance of peace, confidence, and contentment. I could be wrong, but Victoria doesn't strike me as the type to partake in any form of brutal, honest, self-analysis –she's just powering through with relentless bluster, playing the game. The disheartening thing is, she appears to be winning.

It is probably my naivety, but my dream is to carve out the life that I want, and be successful at it, without having to give up my soul; to be just another suit privately yearning for the life of an artist. But in the short term, while Victoria is still based here, I'll play the game too, the best that I can, and try to remain in her good books.

Even if I did have any *real* problems with Victoria, there would be no point in complaining. Victoria is best friends, both inside and outside of work, with all of the people who work in the HR Department, especially the HR Manager, Liz. This leads me to suspect that it would all be a bit of a kangaroo court if I was ever to air any grievances. The two guys that work in our HR department are worse than a man down and besides, they would never have the bottle to cross Liz, the Queen Bee, or Victoria, the new regional big shot.

Joyce teases me by saying that Victoria "holds a candle" for me, but I tell her that it's just Victoria's overly enthusiastic mad face that gives off that impression, Victoria seems too focused on her career to have any time for wild jungle love action with this wee guy.

The overall workforce here is split roughly 50/50 between men and women. However, at my work station I am surrounded by all women, bar Ken. When I first started in here, Ken and I went for a beer, but the relationship has petered out since then. Ken likes to go to the bookies, all he talks about is his punts; on the horses, the dogs, and of course, the football. Just last week he won over a hundred pounds betting on the Luxembourg First Division – he's a betting fiend. At the weekends he plays golf. Golf? Walking about like a prick in a polo shirt, chino slacks, and silly shoes? Nah, not for me. "This guy was under par", "that other guy put the ball in the rough", "this twat said some shite to some bellend in the clubhouse" – sounds like a lot of wank, wrapped in more wank, to me. Visions come to mind of crusty old white men conspiring to reduce the global populous and enslave us all, and doing so, all huckled and decrepit, over a game of fucking golf. "Well, what do *you* like to do at the weekend then Joe, you wee smart arse?" Ken fires back at me, stung by my occasional digs at his pastimes. Oh, he's got me there, "um... eh. We're not talking about me", I reply sheepishly. Ken, all banteriffic, half-serious-half-joking, shuts me right up with, "well, when you stop lounging about your parents' house every weekend in your drawers, scratching your arse, and watching cartoons, then you can come back to me." He's done me there, bravo Ken, you dick.

It would be good to lock into someone else in here, secure in a new solid bromance, or even better, a group bromance. It would help me to forget about the boys; living it up, travelling the world, making memories together. There I go again, self-pitying arse gravy. This needs to stop. For my own good, I need to get over myself, and get over all of this.

CHAPTER 3

I once heard someone say, "tidy house, tidy mind." I don't know if that is a lot of old bollocks or not, but I am willing to give it a try. My bedroom is an absolute disgrace, a complete slap in the chookies to civilised society, no man should live like this. My Mum gave up telling me to clean my room when I was a kid, and despite her relentless requests, it has been a complete midden ever since.

But I am not a kid any more, I am nineteen years old, not thirteen, but you wouldn't think that if you were to walk into my room; you can't see the floor in here, it's that bad. How am I meant to get matters in order when my personal living space looks like this? Clothes and random pish lying everywhere, a shambles really, not to mention all the sexy girl pics all over the walls and ceiling; no nips or hoohahs on show, but plenty of saucy bikini and lingerie shots, that while undeniably mesmeric to look at, I have come to realise are a bit much, a bit too, "one day I hope to touch a real girl." If I ever brought a girl in here, she'd see this madness and probably run a mile. Hopefully, the physical act of cleaning up my room will help to unclutter my mind, be more focused, and enable me to power on, in one way or another.

First job, and it's a biggy – it is even more pressing than taking down all of the sexy lady pics – I need to get rid of all this fucking pornography. It's everywhere in here; mags, VHS tapes, DVDs, and even a pack of playing cards that includes every possible genre of porn; there's even some bestiality shots in there – I have never seen a horse look so happy. One of my mates brought the playing cards back from his football team's tour of Holland. He didn't want to be caught with them in his house, so he thought, "I know, I'll just give them to Joe", and here they have stayed ever since.

The stash started with mags; you buy one, you loan one out, you get a loan of one, then your friends want rid of theirs, so when they offer it to you, you say, "sure, whatever", as you haven't really thought about it either way. It's the same with DVDs and so on; they would come into my possession, I'd forget about them, and only just now have I realised that I have a completely alienating gargantuan pornography stash. I wonder what would happen to me if the police ever found out about this, legal or not. Surely, I would be put straight onto "the database" for this haul, or some kind of a watch-list, at the very least. Even at my age, I know that none of this shit is real, it is a visual stimulant, nothing more. I can only imagine some of the sexual missteps, that must occur all the time, as the result of one person being completely out of kilter during the act, thinking freaky porno is the standard frequency in the act of sex; some poor sort expecting the missionary position and a cuddle, only to be met with some lubed-up freak in nipple clamps and biting on a ball-gag.

Regardless of morality, civic duty, whatever, all I know for certain is that this lot needs putting in a bin bag and left in the woods. Besides, finding "nude books", "jazz mags", or whatever you want to call them, in the woods is a rite of passage for any young boy, whether they are ready for it or not. I am in no doubt, this is a sensitive, potentially volatile, situation, that requires expert attention and *needs* to be handled with secret agent level proficiency and discretion.

I keep my bedroom door ajar, just so that I can hear if either of my parents are coming up the stairs. I start to sift through the chaos of my room, with each row of books I straighten-up on my shelves, I find something. But not only there; the box under my bed, the holdall bag buried at the back of my wardrobe, dodgy discs stashed in CD cases, and then it dawns on me – there's even more than I thought there was, far more. Artefacts of filth can be found in every single nook and cranny of my bedroom. Jesus, there is zero pride in realising that there is enough pornography in here to fill an entire bin bag, to the point where the one bin bag doesn't look as though it will be strong enough to hold the weight, and subsequently, I will have to double bag it.

Daylight is fading, it is almost time. Dad's gone out, I am not sure when he will be home, so I just need to make sure that Mum is kept occupied or this could get very awkward, very quickly. The mere act of me tidying my room would peak her interest alone, such is the novelty, and if she saw me leaving the house with "haul-X", she would undoubtedly ask where I was going, and "what's in the bag?"

Before making my move, I nip downstairs and briefly make small talk with my Mum to try and gain a true sense of her status. Her favourite soap has just started, which is ideal; she'll be glued to this pish for at least fifteen minutes or so until the ad break, when she'll get up from her chair to go and make a cup of tea. I mumble to my Mum that I am nipping out for a walk, to which she replies, without breaking her glaze from the TV, "that's nice son. You relax and enjoy your stroll." I close the living room door, I turn and bolt straight up the stairs, snatch the bag, before bombing right back down the stairs again, before finally bursting out the front door – a man on a mission.

I make my way over the hill across from our house, past the wooden park bench and the old oak tree, it's not too far a distance to the dirt track that leads through the woods. The pavement ends at the shin-high fence at the entry way of where the dirt path starts, I take one quick look to see who or what is around me, the coast is clear. All I need to do is make it deep into the woods and toss my big ol' bag of porn away and stage one of "Operation Life Clean-Up" will be complete. I'm trying my best to not look like a right shifty character but I suspect my body language betrays me. I hastily stride through the woods, it's getting dark, but not quite dark enough. This place can be busy with dog walkers and random passers-by, so I am delighted to find that it is as quiet as a graveyard.

The further I walk, and without seeing anyone, the more I begin to relax and wonder what all the fuss was about. I get to what must be roughly the half way point, to where I see a plentiful bunch of bushes, and I think, "XXX marks the spot!" I throw the bag down. That was easy. Job done. But there is just one thing, I have the bladder of a five year old, and in all of the excitement, I need a wicked pee. Feeling emboldened; no one is here, the drop-off had gone without a hitch. I decide to just get my nudger out and pee where I stand, nature to nature and all that. So, out we get. It's a full throttle one, real power-hose stuff, I must have been needing that, one of those long, really satisfying pees; like the kind of piss that borders on orgasmic after having been stuck on a long bus journey.

I am peeing for so long that I start to aim it in shapes on the long grass, I come to the end and let out an almighty "ahhh", such is the feel good factor of being free from such a urinary burden. But then I hear this rustling sound. I turn around and standing not far from me is this wee wirey middle-aged man holding a dog leash, the kind of man that has the build, and the air bout him, that he was perhaps a boxer in his day.

I don't know how long he was watching me pee, regardless, his expression is of complete disgust, that much is for sure. For a brief moment, we just stare at each other – it is so surreal, here I am in the woods with my tadge and freaky pubes hanging out, getting eye-balled by some strange wee guy, with neither of us saying a word to each other. This is so intense, he's breathing strongly through his nostrils, his jaw clenched tight, it's obvious that he's clearly furious. Something has got to give. He slowly turns his head to the side, and oh shit! He sees the bag.

As quick as a cat he pounces forward towards the bag, snatching at it with his fingers, all extended and fierce like claws, and although it is double bagged, he bursts the bag immediately – dirty mags come bundling out; like gold coins in some treasure laden booby trap. Finally, the silence is broken when he looks straight at me and barks, "dirty... wee... bastard!" He is trembling with rage, his fists clenched. If I thought he shouted at me loudly there, then what was to follow was on a completely other level. "DIRTY WEE BASTARD!!!" The unholy decibel level of his hardened voice rings through me.

Fuck this, I'm off! I start running as fast as I can, I don't even have time to zip myself up. My adrenaline is through the roof, it's primal, a sensation that speaks to me saying, "this is real you wee fanny, you are in a really hairy situation here and you're just going to have to deal with it." I haven't felt a jolt to my system like this since I was last in a fight, and that was over a decade ago. Jesus, I didn't know that I could run this fast, because before I know it, I am clear of the woods already.

Still running at full pace, I turn my head for a moment to see if I have out ran him, holy fuck! The wee guy is only about 10ft, 15ft tops, behind me. Who is this old-school, cyborg, dog walking, vigilante, angry mad fucker? When he sees me glancing back at him, he yells when he can, in short bursts; through his heavy breathing, "disgusting... bastard... pervert!"

Despite being right in the middle of an intense on-foot pursuit, the weight of just how bad this could get suddenly dawns on me; he could catch me and batter lumps out of me, but far worse; I was standing in a public place, exposed, with a large bag of porn. If he was to report me, this is a small town, rumours would surely run wild – "kids play there", "he had porn", then that would mutate into "he had kid porn", which would then twist further into "he had his dick out to kid porn in the woods." So many potential monumentally horrific accusations, when all I wanted was to be rid of a colossal porn stash that I had slept walked into possessing. Then it dawns on me, why didn't I just throw it in the bin? No one would have seen what was in the bag, had I just put in a wheely bin or taken it to the town dump. Just because I had found porn in the woods when I was a kid did not mean that younger kids now had to find mine, I could have played my part in ending the porn discovery cycle, it could have been the birth of an environmentally friendly, jazz mag disposal revolution. But no, here I am flirting with disaster, with my frightened dong waving in the wind.

Got to keep running, got to make sure that no matter what happens I don't get caught. I am now running through the streets, dangerously close to where I live. If anyone sees me, it's game over, so I decide to make my way towards more unfamiliar streets, the further away from home, the better. As uncomfortable as it is, mid-sprint, I shove my piece back in my jeans.

I run and run and run, I take another look around and thankfully, this time, at last, the man chasing me is now a small figure in the distance and the dog that he was walking has appeared and is running alongside him. Luckily, his dog is a small yappy little creature. The man stops, leans forward, clearly exhausted, he places his hands on his knees, looking up he shouts at me, "your card's marked son!" Before letting out one final, "bastard!"

Despite me breathing out of my arse, I continue running at a decent pace until there is almost no chance that he would catch up with me. I wait another hour or so until it is completely dark and strategically make my way home. Absolutely knackered, I park my bum on the bench by the oak tree, that sits on the hill in front of my house. I'm absolutely soaked through with sweat. Nearly out-ran by a man three times my age, what a wake-up call.

I am still breathing really heavily, I cannot believe how out of shape I am. It takes me a few minutes to ease my heart rate down and breathe semi-normally. Despite my sweatiness, I can't be bothered moving, but sooner or later I know I will have to, I can't just sit here all night because I am lazy. "You alright there young man?" Jesus, I get the fright of my life. You would think that seeing as I had just been chased, my senses would be heightened and working overtime, but no, I turn around to see an elderly man sat on the end of the park bench, I didn't hear him approaching me at all. "You're looking a bit pasty there son, are you feeling alright?" Somewhat embarrassed at the state of me, I reply, "eh, I was out running." Clearly confused, the old man replies, "out running, with your denims on?" I would like to be honest with this old dude, but I think that I will refrain from telling him about my flirtation with being caught, beaten, and prosecuted for public indecency, exposure, and any other charge they could possibly throw at me. I mumble, "eh, I went for a walk. And half way through I decided to just start running, and here I am." The old fella doesn't look entirely convinced. "Well – I can't say that I am surprised. You young ones these days, I can't make head nor tail of you." The old boy then just sits there in silence, staring outward, with a satisfied expression on his face. He has an assured presence about him; he sits upright with his back straight, like he is proud, and he appears completely comfortable in the quietness.

I have had enough awkwardness for the night, not to mention bizarre encounters with strange old men, probably best to nip this in the bud. "Oh well, I better be going now", I say sharply as I stand up. He replies, "sure thing kiddo, you get yourself up the road, and have yourself a good warm shower." In that couple of seconds since I stood up, I feel the cold breeze travel right down my sweat soaked back. I reply to the old gent, "I will do. See you around I guess." The old man gives me a firm acknowledging nod of the head before I start walking, making my way down the hill towards my house.

I open the front door of my house to a wall of sound, coming from whatever pish Mum is watching on the TV. Dad comes down the stairs with a passing, "hi son." I say, "alright Dad" back to him, as he makes his way through to the kitchen. Now a bag of porn lighter, I walk slowly upstairs to my room, I shut the door behind me. Once closed, I lean my head against it and close my eyes. Right, tonight was a close call, but I'll have to take the positives from it –

the most important thing is that the stash is gone, never to return.

Plus, there was a bonus cardio workout flung in there for good

measure. It didn't go as planned, by any means; I'm frazzled and I

smell like a yeti. It wasn't easy. But then again, what is?

CHAPTER 4

It's time, time to reconnect with the world, time to be reborn. There aren't any guys from work that I could see myself hanging around with, and although there are a handful of guys that I could probably have a laugh with that drink down my local pub, there are certain substance issues that put me off. It's not a sense of righteousness that stops me from socialising down the pub, but I have to call a spade a spade, when I say that they've all pretty much become sweaty, clawing, coke-headed fuckwits. They're old enough to know what they are doing, it's their choice, and I can't say that there have not been times when I have been tempted and a tad curious, but bum tickers run in my family; I don't want to be a sweat-soaked gibbering mess at 4am on a Sunday morning, when my heart explodes and sprays out of my ears, nose, and arse. Even if I thought I could handle taking it, there would be that grim knowing that I was clinging on to the faintest sense of connection or comradery; unsure if I was really liked, or just another mug, a ten-a-penny sucker in the shit-show of modern drug culture. Also, I couldn't afford it even if I wanted it, and by all accounts the boys from the boozer go deep with that nasty shit. It is bizarre; it always seemed like the boys just enjoyed having a few beers, and then, boom! Cocaine had arrived. Even some of the old bar flies have had a dabble. The prospect of dying young needlessly, or having to deal with shadey pusher types with tattooed necks, it just isn't for me – I don't care what anyone says, a tattoo on your neck is a bold statement by anyone's standards, and anyone who gets one is for the watching. Haha, and here I was, trying not to sound righteous.

There has to be another way to meet people that I have a chance of getting along with, that share a mutual interest. I love films, I could start a film club, and each week we could watch one together and then sit around and chat about it. Then we could talk about upcoming films, film trivia, all sorts of quality geekary and outright bumphery until the cows came home. But then again, there is no way that Dad would ever allow random folk to sit about our house; on our couches, using up his electricity to waste time bullshitting about films, so really this film club pish is a bit of a non-starter. However, a book club might be the answer, all we would need for that is a room, some chairs, and some light. Dad never uses the garage; he would take his car to the local mechanic to change a headlight bulb. The garage, as things stand, is more like a glorified storage cupboard filled with nothing but junk. If I were to pitch it to my Dad that I was tidying it up so that I could have some friends over to just sit around in, away from the house, I am sure that he would at least consider it.

Luckily for me, he agreed, but first I had to spend the best part of a week cleaning the place out. There was all manner of shite in there, for example; three broken VCRs and a large print of the Golden Gate Bridge. So strange, especially when you consider that I do not know of anyone that either I, or my family, know, who has ever even been to San Francisco. I think my Dad must have bought it in the early 1980's after going to see "A View to a Kill." Dad was always a Roger Moore man, and although enjoying his Bond films, I am a Connery man all of the way; a national acting icon, top shagger too I suspect. What was even more bizarre, was that when I took the print of the Golden Gate Bridge to the local dump, the guy who worked there looked me up and down aggressively, his brow furrowed, as if to say, "what are you doing with a picture of some fancy American bridge? Ya wee dick." I guess he's more of an old TV and fridge kind of Midge Man.

Having gotten rid of all the junk, swept the floor, and plugged in a couple of air fresheners, the garage actually looked, and smelled, pretty decent. Now all I had to do was target people who might be interested in coming along.

I went down to the local supermarket and put an ad on the general information board, and while I was there I bought a cheap kettle, one packet each of bourbons and custard creams biscuits, some cheap cups, tea bags, and a small jar of expensive coffee – high quality jars of coffee, and bin bags, are the only two items on Earth that you should never scrimp on.

From there I went to the local library. I was going to pop by my old church and leave an advertising card on their events board, but after mulling it over, I came to the conclusion that it would probably be best not to, I don't want to run the risk of someone who used to see me there every week being at my new club, I am trying to leave all of that behind. It's just not for me anymore.

On each card that I placed on the various notice boards around town, I highlight that the first meeting takes place a week on Wednesday, that all are welcome, my address details, and my first name. I don't give out my telephone number or email address, to avoid being harassed by pranking nob-jockies. In the ad, I try to set the right tone, I do my best to word it in such a way that the invitation comes off as light, friendly, and devoid of stiffness. However, upon reflection I am pretty sure I used the phrase "we can meet and chat", which very much sounds like a line from one of those late night dating commercials. I don't want to be mercilessly bum-dungeoned by a local tramp, I am just looking to meet some new people, build some kind of network, hopefully strike up a rapport, and maybe make some new friends. Since the band imploded I have been quite hard on myself, this whole time I have been feeling like a dumb shit, a bit of a clown. So deep down, I am hoping that if people come along to my book club, they'll think, "this guy reads, he must be intelligent. He bought biscuits and made us coffee, he must be a nice guy." Haha, the desperation is ripping out of me.

Wednesday evening comes around and no one has come, not a soul. I am sat in my garage with nothing better to do than just stare at the two packets of biscuits that I bought especially for this occasion. I keep telling myself that it will all be alright, that people must just be running late, and that they will surely be here any minute now. Then the "what ifs" kick in. I should have put something online, people of all ages are online these days, sure I didn't want to be bombarded with mortgage deals and penis enlargement pill ads, but I could have quickly syphoned them away with my trusty email junk filter. I stated in the ad that the meeting would start at 19:00, it's 19:20 now. Maybe the wording wasn't clear, I stated, "Meeting is on from 19:00 – 21:00, feel free to pop by any time." I guess I should have worded it so that people knew to be here as early as possible.

It's now 20:20, a big part of me wants to cry then wreck the place, but despite these extreme underlying emotions, I can't help but laugh. The sheer absurdity of it all; trying to make a connection, fling a little "I'm here you bastards" out into the universe and see what comes back, and failing miserably. What a shit show, back to the drawing board I suppose.

20:35, still no one here. Fuck it, the bourbons are getting cracked open, I might as well go down with a sugar high, send my insulin levels up to Pluto. I eat two biscuits so quickly I practically inhale them, such measly sugary consolation, such fleeting mouth pleasure. Then suddenly, I feel this searing pain in my eye. A small bit of dust or something has found its way under my contact lens. Luckily, I have my trusty contact lenses case in my pocket, so I quickly take my lenses out and put them in their solution. Ah, it's such a relief to get them out at the best of times, but especially when there's a bit of dirt in there, as it may as well be a fish hook. The garage is now a blur, I park my bum down on a chair and begin to rub my eyes. I take a deep breath, there's no point sitting around here all night, alone and munching biscuits like some big comfort-eating sad-case dildo.

Best thing I can do is just put the biscuits down, put out the lights, and go to bed. But I'm still not moving, my arse stays firmly planted – the failure of tonight's event has left me feeling really deflated, it has been a good old kick in the chooks. I'm torn, do I really want to go to bed and lie in the dark and micro analyse the disappointment of tonight's non-event, and how much of a tit I feel? "Hello" - I spring to my feet, who is this? A voice, coming from outside. "Is there anyone there? I am here for the book club." Holy shit! A female voice, coming from the other side of the garage door, and she doesn't sound like anyone from around here, it's a soft European accent, but I am not sure straight away. As it is dark outside, her presence has triggered the security lights at the back of my house. I don't even think to quickly pop my contact lenses back in. I lean forward to lift up the garage door and there in the beaming light is the blurred silhouette of a slim, presumably young, woman. Is she an angel? An alien? An alien angel? Why did I have to take my lenses out, of all the times to have dirt in my eye. I raise my hand above my eyes to protect them from the glare of the security lights, when the mystery girl enquires, "Joe?" I clear my throat and I reply in my best Scottish person on TV voice. "Yes, I am Joe, that's me." She moves a half-step closer, such is my shitty eye-sight I can just make out that she is looking passed my shoulders to enquire where everyone else is. "I am here for the book club. I am sorry that I am so late. I thought that I would come by and introduce myself and find out what I should read for the next meeting." Ooft. That sting, it is such a raw aching sensation to have to tell some girl, on the first time of meeting her, that you tried to put something together, and it completely fell on its arse at the first hurdle. "I'm sorry. I am afraid that no one showed up. Well, apart from you." We both pause for a moment in awkward silence, and in those strained few seconds it dawns on me that even with my eye condition, keritoconis, skewing my eye balls, and turning my sight to dog shit, this girl is the most beautiful blur I have ever seen. The girl replies politely, "oh, I am sorry to hear that. It was nice to meet you Joe. Bye-bye." Her simply saying "nice to meet you" sends a lightning bolt through me. Jesus, how needy am I? She turns and starts to walk away, when I blurt out, "wait!" "Yes?" she replies inquisitively. Slightly more measured, and not quite as desperate sounding, I tell her, "eh, thanks for coming." She pauses in silent acknowledgment, turns, and walks from the searing brightness of the security lights into the darkness of the unlit driveway.

Just for a moment, the smell of the oil and dampness of the garage fades and this subtle, yet completely intoxicating, scent of perfume consumes my nostrils. It's glorious, I just want to hold on to it, I don't want to breathe it back out. Right, bollocks to this, enough of my shit. I am going straight up the stairs, washing my contact lenses, and getting my running clothes on. I need to get in shape, I can't be some self-pitying, biscuit munching, garage dwelling bastard if I am ever to stand a chance with a girl like her. I guess tonight was not a complete disaster after all, meeting her has given me the jolt I needed. It's time to scrub my balls, both literally and metaphorically, and sharpen up.

CHAPTER 5

Monday morning's back again. I need to start afresh and not approach my working life like I have been doing; such a negative attitude; get up, drive to work, log in, zone out. I have been a walking talking miserable-guy-who-works-in-an-office-cubicle cliché.

However, this morning I got up a bit earlier, I shaved, and spent the extra time required to make sure that my shirt was the most ironed any of my shirts have ever been. It is time to dress for the job I want, and not the job I have, and although I don't know what job I want, it will do me no harm to make more of an effort with my appearance.

I make my way out of the house and get into my car. Immediately, as I open the door I notice a real whiff that I hadn't previously, it gets me thinking that I really should buy an air freshener for in here too — it smells of motor oil and dog farts, and I don't even own a dog, regardless, it's fucking honking. I put the key in the ignition, sub-consciously haughty and entitled that the car should, and will, immediately fire into action and I can be on my way. But not today cock master!

With each turn of the key, there is this "fuh fuh fuh fuh" noise. My immediate reaction is to yell at the car as if it were sentient, "no! Work, start you bastard, work!" Turning the ignition, again and again, there's nothing doing, it's like when you hit an air-shot at football; that maddening frustration, looking like a complete diddy. I just keep repeating to myself aloud, "come on, come on."

Someone's having a laugh here, it's now no longer even making the "fuh fuh fuh fuh" failing noise, it's dead, dead as absolute fuck. Is the ignition gubbed? Has the battery gone to pure mince? There could be a problem with the flumboid-conjunctor-mobulater for all I know, it's all a fucking mystery. Oh bollocks, my cat has a better knowledge of cars than me, there really is no point in popping the bonnet to see if I can do anything. I can drive a car, that's it; the internal aspects of any motor vehicle may as well be made up of pixie dust, candyfloss, and good intentions for all the good that it will do me. It took me four attempts to pass my driving test, and such was that sense of fiasco that it sickened me into not caring to learn anything more than the basics; like checking tyre pressure and oil levels – everything else is for the people down at the car mechanics; real people, grown up people.

The bus it is. I am not the biggest fan of taking the bus to be honest. I like to get to where I am going, not having to stop at forty places in between. Plus, often my guts feel like warm soup in a tumble dryer, such is my proneness to travel sickness. I think it's the heat; if it is warm outside the air conditioning is non-existent, and if it's cold everyone closes the window while the driver turns the heating up full blast. I have nearly yacked into a few woolly hats in my time due to riding in roasting hot buses on cold days. I thought that once I got my car, my days on the buses were over, forever and ever, amen.

I power-walk to the bus stop, catching my bus with only a few seconds to spare, the number 22. To my complete surprise, the seats are really comfy, so comfy that I can feel myself falling asleep. Drifting off, I think about the girl with the, what I think is a, French accent, the only person to show up for my book club. Oh yes – may the universe drench my brain with lovely endorphins, brought about by the sweetest dreams of her. I instantly fall into a deep sleep, I must be, as I am dreaming straight away, and it is crystal clear, as I can hear her, her soft lovely accent. It is like she is asking me a question about something, and I can't help but be completely attentive to her. But wait, what? What is going on? Is she talking to me in a dream, or am I just imagining it, or is she really here? I am teetering in that grey area – the confusing throes between dream state and full consciousness, when I finally realise, "hold on, wake up! It's her!" And it is.

There she is, stood at the front of the bus asking the driver for some information as she points to a diagram of the bus route, that is situated on a panel by the door, "so, I get off here to get the transfer to the airport?" It's her, it's her! Asking the driver about the airport, I think to myself, "don't go there you lovely, lovely person, stay here." She steps off of the bus and pauses for a moment to fasten the top button of her long red coat, and put her hat on, a little black beret none the less. For the first time, I see her face. Holy. Shit. She's beautiful; long brown hair, high cheek bones, and big hypnotising blue eyes.

God bless my contact lenses. When I first saw her blurry outline, and heard that accent, I was smitten, but now that I have seen her properly – she is just gorgeous – blessed with the kind of beauty that is so mesmerising, so enchanting, so foreign, and ultimately, so utterly unobtainable. Brain suitably foggy, I will probably be moosh all day now.

But wait, she was heading to the airport. She didn't have any luggage with her, so chances are she's going to meet someone. I hope it's not some huge donged love connection – that would just not do. Once again, who am I trying to kid? Of course, she's off to meet some stunt-shagger, a girl like that could never be single. Well, not for long anyway.

But what are the chances of meeting her last night for the first time, and then seeing her again this morning? I never take the bus. It probably isn't, but it could be fate. This taking the bus malarkey could have something to it after all; I am probably damned forever now to hopelessly take the number 22 bus back and forth in the vain hope of seeing her again.

She is so attractive that I just want to learn to cook; take up kayaking, learn Japanese, anything, anything at all to give me any kind of edge, to somehow catch her eye. I can't ask a girl like that back to mine, when all I have to offer her is some tea and toast, and watching "Thunder Cats" on VHS. I will need to meet her again and try and frame myself in some way that she does not run away immediately. It is absolute madness, that such a nothing moment has charged me right up again – she didn't even see me, never mind send some shine my way. Regardless, it feels good just to have the dust blown off my joy receptors.

I arrive at work with this stupid big grin on my face – the mere sight of her, finally getting to see her lovely chops, and hearing that accent, it really has put a spring in my step. And to top it all off, despite my car dying on me, not only am I not late for work, I am ten minutes early.

There's time to check my emails and see if there is anything interesting in my inbox other than the usual work related dung; like HR reminding everyone on the reinforcement of the no jeans policy, Harry from upstairs looking for people to sponsor his paraglide in aid of dogs with diabetes, and some sort who I haven't heard of before trying to arrange a team building day out, go-karting none the less. Brrrrr, I shudder at the thought, I would rather be flung in an industrial microwave, wrapped in tinfoil, and have the power set to the ultimate maximus − if there is anything worse than no fun, it's corporate approved forced fun.

However, despite my lack of appetite for work sanctioned play time, there is an email about a charity telethon being held in here shortly; it takes place after hours, and I have heard that it is usually a good laugh. It won't cost me anything, it's only for a couple of hours, it's for a good cause, and I don't need to go anywhere for it − I can participate while being sat at my own desk, on my wee chunky bahooki. Plus, you are allowed to bring friends, so there will be a lot of non-worky folk there to meet, and at the very least, look at through my perviscope.

Other than that fluff, there's not too much going on in my inbox. And then I see it, an email from Trumpet with the subject "Alright". How did he even get my work email address? Mum must have given it to his Mum, I guess. Do I open it? I'm not sure that I'm ready for this shit. It's got me rattled; like a creepy finger shoved up my phantom zone, or a message from beyond the grave; the Ghost-of-Pals-Gone-to-Absolute-Fuck-past. The email reads:

Joe

I know things got a bit messed up and some things were said in anger and all that. But we're mates...

We all think that it's water under the bridge. Drop us a line, it doesn't have to be like this.

I hope you are cool.

Trumpet

Pfft. That eh, that hurts, as in the emotional anguish of just reading that actually has a real physical effect on me; like a kick in the balls, combined with a kidney jab, and a poke in the eye for good measure. Here I was on this high of finally seeing my dream girl's face, who I met last night for the first time, and sure, I'm a fucking nutter and nothing will come of this, but at least I could bask in my own delusion. How fragile that bubble must have been, that this one poxy pissing email sinks me, aided by the reservoir of old shit that I carry deep inside me.

I can't reply to him, not him, or any one of them for that matter. There's been too much said and too much time has passed. The longer it goes on, the bigger and deeper it all gets. We had never fallen out before. and when we did, it felt nuclear, and I just don't know if I have it in me to try and patch things up. It would probably take some kind of outer body experience to broach it all. I think I will just stew in this a little longer. I choose to hide from any further emails from Trumpet by directing his email address to my account's junk filter — If only I hadn't read that, I could have stayed on that high, if only for a wee bit longer.

CHAPTER 6

Sat in our living room, the entire sofa to myself, Dad on his arm chair, Mum pottering around; tidying, re-tidying, busying herself however she can, and Golf is on the TV. Part of me suspects that, given my presence, my Dad thinks that I may, finally, be getting into Golf. But what my mother fucker needs to know is – rock stars don't golf.

I haven't put my lenses in yet this morning, staring at the screen, it's just one big green blur. Without the ability to focus, it is not long until I am day dreaming – my mind drifting to how I no longer return to what was once my reoccurring dream about me flying. That dream seems to have vanished, hiding in the deep obscure recesses of my brain, from whence it came. My dreams are now pretty much all anxiety based; angry figures demanding that I speak, but I have no mouth; all I can offer are strange moaning sounds, and the louder and louder I get, before finally, I wake up, sure that I will be sick, swallow my own tongue, or die of a heart attack.

My Dad and I sit in silence, the fact is – we have fuck all to say to each other. Somewhere along the line, he didn't care to hear any of my shite any more, and the feeling was mutual. It's not a nasty thing, there's no passive aggression, it's a relaxed acceptance that despite me spawning from the depths of his man satchel, our shared DNA has not transpired into mutual interests. I am totally cool with it; there's absolutely no point in trying to frame it in my mind as a hurtful thing, it is what it is.

But as we sit here, perhaps, just maybe, my Dad is secretly pleased that I am taking in the golf. However, he has no idea, that firstly, I don't have my lenses in and can't see shit, and that also, my real motivation is to intercept the mail when it arrives before either my Mum or Dad have the chance to see it.

Waiting, the posty should be here any minute. For a second, I look away from the TV and conduct one of my occasional sight tests; having such poor vision, every now and then, I pan around to see if I can see anything even remotely clearly, and if I can, I try to work out why that and not everything else. Scanning the room, it's just the usual; blurred outlines, no real detail of anything. Although, there is a beam of light shining through from the patio doors in the dining room, all the way through to the living room, and where it stops is the front of my Dad's wee baldy dome. There, as if highlighted in perfect illumination by the Lord himself, I can see a handful of baby arse hairs stranded on the horizon of pure shineyness, that is my father's head. The only thing we will eventually have in common will be my auld man bestowing me with male pattern baldness, his one true legacy. Perhaps me getting into so much debt and potentially destroying my family's credit record is the Universe's way of punishing my Dad for cursing me with decades of being a complete cone head. I wish that he would wet shave those creepy wee hairs off, they look like little zombie corpses, only half risen from the grave.

I snap out of my baldness pondering when, as the living room is right next to the front door, I hear the letterbox open, then the subtle bump of mail hitting the floor. Either Dad didn't hear it, or he's not overly fussed at the prospect of reading his mail, but I am. I rise from the couch and open the door into the hall, I reach down and snatch up the mail, there are four letters, I immediately seek out the privacy of our downstairs toilet. This is what my parents are oblivious to; that I am only loitering about the living room to ensure that neither of them see the scary looking letters from the credit card companies. Daft boy, I really should have put my lenses in for this; I hold the letters right up to my face – the first letter is for Dad, but the following three are for me, all of which, to varying terrifying degrees, basically say, "give us our fucking money back!"

Like in the Book of Genesis, just as God had fashioned Adam from dust, I wanted to fashion a new creation; a new reality of boundless opportunities for myself, doing what I loved the most, but not from dust, but hard plastic. And like the tale of Adam and Eve, I too was tempted by a serpent; the blood sucking unholy creature that is quick and easy credit, and although it hasn't happened yet, similarly, I face the distinct possibility of banishment also. The harsh reality is, if I can't turn this tide, and this mountain of shit topples down on me, there is every chance that my parents will kick me out on the streets. I can't get it out of my head; this chilling desperate fear that when this has all fully unfolded and there is no more wiggle room for negotiation or reparation, it could see me homeless.

Life on the streets would fucking annihilate me, I am soft as shite. There, I said it.

And like some kind of serpent, I feel as though a big horrible snake bastard; like a boa constrictor or a python, has thrown coils around my body, squeezing the air from my lungs completely, such is the sense of fear and anxiety consuming me.

I need to exercise, I need to get my body and head right. I need to investigate what financial guidance is available, if there even is any, and bit by bit, chip away at this. Basically, I need to stop hiding and burying my head in the sand and start facing up to this. I am shite with numbers, that's a given, it just means that I will have to work twice as hard to get myself back on track. The key thing that I need to ensure stays solid, is my job; having an income, as low as it may be, will be the core of my financial redemption. I must take ownership of this, I cannot, CANNOT, labour my poor folks with this mad bullshit – we might not be a TV family, or have anything in common, but they are good people, they don't deserve it.

I fold the letters and place them in my back pocket. My eyes coated in the faintest layer of moisture; not quite tears, but getting there. I go upstairs and put the letters with the rest of them, in an old shoe box on the top shelf of my wardrobe. I'll get my running gear on and go a run. When I get back, I'll see if I can get on the PC and start researching a way to dig myself out of this. I'll be sure to delete the cookies and the browser history to cover my tracks – if only Dad would do that now and then, there are only so many Asian Babe websites that I feel I can handle, the old dog that he is.

CHAPTER 7

Stretch, that's the one thing that I remember the PE teachers at school telling us that we had to do before any kind of physical activity. Here I am, stretching out and warming up all of my unit the best I know how, getting ready, ready to just get in amongst it and blow those lungs of mine wide open. I have prepared as best I can; bountiful blasts of talcum powder have been applied to my inner thighs and scrotal sector to avoid chafing and I have successfully dispatched a pre-run sheizer; just like my gigging days, I can't be running about with a power-log half hanging out of me. With all of the points on my physical preparation to-do list successfully ticked, I now have to make sure that I will be mentally prepared, and that means making sure that I have my MP3 player. It is fully charged and stocked with the right kind of music; this is not the time for mopey, heart-string pulling, contemplative, acoustic shit. I need the real stuff; upbeat, fast tempo songs, with killer bass and melt-your-face drum work. I am going to just get out there, beast my system, come home, have a shower, and then, I will be prepared to conduct a full online investigation into what I can do to stop my financial rot.

I set off, and pleasantly the first five minutes or so are not too bad. But without any gradual transitional period, my physical state descends into an intestinal reshuffle of sorts, and very quickly, it is apparent that I am well and truly gubbed. I feel just as unfit as when I was being chased by the dog walker, on the night of "Nude-book-Gate", the key difference being that right now I am lacking a spike of adrenalin, the kind that only comes when you are being pursued on foot by a furious man armed with a dog leash, who mistakenly perceives you to be a maniacal public sex pervert.

This is brutal, absolutely horrible. Why is it that having a few beers, parked on your arse, watching TV, comes at such a cost? A few take-away curries, some crisps watching the football – the short lived gratification, it simply is not worth this running palaver. Although, despite my sluggishness, I must not stop, even though I want to, and I mean, I *really* want to, more than anything. I ate some cereal around an hour ago, I'm not sure if enough essential digestion time has elapsed; I let out a few danger burps, the cereal is affecting me. But it doesn't stop there, in the hellish hairy sweaty nightmare that is my ring-piece I can feel an almighty trouser-cough brewing, my pre-run sheizer has not saved me as much as I thought it would have. I take a quick look around me to see if there is anyone around. No angry dog walkers this time, so I relax and let out a horrid sneaker. It makes my stomach feel better but it causes a brief moment of concern when I teeter dangerously close to following through. A key step on the road to self-esteem, "Joe, be sure to not take a shit on the pavement", I tell myself reassuringly, moderately confident in the functioning capabilities of my sphincter.

The target is to keep on running until I make it back to the bench on the hill across from my house. Eventually I see the bench, it looks glorious, I cannot wait to park my sweaty wee rump on it and put an end to this madness. I know that you are meant to do a warm down, but that sounds like crazy bullshit to me, that can wait for when I have been doing this regularly and built up a tolerance. My breathing; I'm borderline hyperventilating but it can only get better from here on in, or then again, I could drop down stone dead. I could be sick, most certainly I could, if I really wanted to, but I don't want to; "casual vomiting", I never really conquered it as an art form. I tend to be in the "please, for the love of God, put me out of my misery and shoot me right now, rather than throw up" camp. I just need to ride this wave, regulate my breathing, and focus on not keeling over and/or dying. I'm such a sweaty mess, but in an almost sadomasochistic way it feels good; like I am sweating all of the horrible toxins out of me; the microwave burgers, the cheap packets of noodles, the supermarket beer, and most importantly, alleviating the stress. I close my eyes for just a second, a breeze blows by, that combined with the sweat on my brow, it cools me down quite considerably. It feels amazing, such a comforting, natural sensation. I think that I am growing fond of sitting on this bench, as once again in quick succession I am so tired and spaced out that I think that I could just fall asleep right here, no problem at all. It's so quiet and still, all I can hear is the gentle rustle of the wind through the leaves of the old oak tree.

"Good evening son". I open my eyes and turn to see that sat next to me again is the older gent that I met the night that I got chased. It amuses me that I didn't see or hear him sitting next to me, for the second time in a row. "You again? You could be an assassin with those twinkly toes of yours." The old man smiles wryly, "how do you know that I am not one?" If I am ever to be "taken out", I would rather it wasn't by an OAP – there is zero credibility in death via the elderly. "Out running again I see. At least this time you were sensible and dressed appropriately", he tells me, clearly breaking my balls. I smile and nod, to acknowledge that he is right, and let him know that I am taking his comments as good natured ribbing. Offering his hand to shake, "by the way, we've not been properly introduced. My name is Walter." I return the gesture, warning him, "excuse my sweaty mitt. Pleased to meet you Walter, I'm Joe." Walter takes back his hand, clearly unperturbed by my sweat soaked hand, and faces forward as he tells me, "Joe eh? I like that name, Joe's a good name." Walter continues, "good to see you out exercising. I wish I could still run about like that but I'm too old now, walking is my thing, I walk everywhere. During my walks, I always pause for a wee five minute rest on this bench, been coming here for years now, since way back before any of these houses were built." Surprised, I ask him, "for years? I live just down there at No.1 and, until last week, I don't recall having ever seen you before." Very matter of fact, Walter replies. "Well, I have." Then silence. I'm happy enough sitting in silence with this old boy – I am too tired to fabricate sparks of small talk, or be perturbed by the lack of it.

I close my eyes again for a micro-second before Walter pipes up, "I wouldn't sit about here much longer if I were you Joe, your muscles will seize up, best to head in and freshen up. I first learned that during the war. Besides, you're stinking." I can't help but laugh, this guy's a character. "You've got me there Walter. When you're right, you're right. You enjoy the rest of your walk." Walter, very self-assured, replies, "certainly."

I stand up, my body begins to ache as I've stiffened up. "Well, it was nice meeting you again, and getting formally introduced this time Walter. Probably see you about." And without missing a beat, Walter simply replies "maybe son, maybe."

I get home, and go for a nice hot shower. Mum and Dad have gone to bed slightly earlier than normal. I boot up the PC and grab a note pad and pen. I am hoping that I can find something online that can give me a bit of guidance and minimise the pain of all this.

CHAPTER 8

It is the night of the telethon. Just before I leave the house, I notice my Fender Strat guitar, the one that I bought myself with the credit cards. I have no idea as to when was the last time that I played it; covered in dust and almost certainly out of tune, it serves as a toxic reminder of the genesis of my debt, and although I should probably sell it, it breaks my heart to know that I would get a fraction of what I paid for it. I should have stuck to my tried and tested, old rickety Fender copy that I grew up with – that I gave away, thinking that I was too good for it. No point dwelling on it any further, it's time to catch the bus.

I would usually be the designated driver on nights like this; but seeing as I currently have no mates and my car is completely goosed, I feel like blowing off a little steam – the Universe is declaring beers. However, such are my funds, it is unlikely that I personally will donate anything in terms of cold hard cash to the telethon – I will be giving up a few hours of my time, before spending the little money that I do have in the pub later on tonight. I guess that I will justify spending my doe on beer, rather than donate it to charity, by deluding myself that for tonight I will be facilitating the generation of funds for the sick and the vulnerable, just not with *my* money. Hopefully, sooner rather than later, when I sort out my finances I will give to charity, but not now, not when I am in this farce; this self-inflicted muddle.

I have been told that when we host charity nights like this, the majority of calls are quite chirpy; as it is people looking to donate to worthy causes. Happy people phoning in is the complete opposite to the insurance claim calls I handle in my day-to-day in work; people in distress, frantically detailing their very own tale of personal carnage and bad luck, as I run through my script of, what must be infuriating and often completely irrelevant, mandatory questions. Plus, it is nice to see people from work in their civilian clothing, it's humanising to see senior management, who ordinarily dress with all the charm and warmth of the Third Reich, in Dad jeans and bright coloured polo shirts. Plus, I got here early enough that I managed to ensure that I got to sit at my own desk, as apparently it is usually a free for all with regards to where you get to sit.

The only thing that I am a bit miffed at, is that they have taken away all of the peds from under the desks, which is a bit of a bummer as I had planned to rifle through my supplies to see if there were any treats to munch on between calls. Besides, I am off for a week on annual leave after tonight, so it's a nice way to cap things off as I ease into seven days away from the office. I had to take my annual leave now or I would lose it, but I have nothing planned, apart from maybe going into the city to see if I can get an appointment with the Citizens Advice Bureau, to find out if they can assist me with my predicament. Regardless, I will need to find something to keep me occupied, something constructive. I never thought the day would come, but my days of just lying in bed all day, furiously wanking in between multiple naps, just for the sake of it, are over. This bit of time off will give me an opportunity to think things through and strategise my comeback from the brink.

I am told that most people bring a friend or relative to help out at these charity events, but who would I bring along? Walter? The old boy that I have met twice, who is about seventy years older than me? Then again, why not? The harsh reality is that he's the closest thing that I have right now to a friend and I am really in no position to be snotty about anything, especially when it comes to relationships of any kind. Besides, Walter would probably charm the socks off the people on the phone and have them pledging away all their money. Maybe next year, if we are both still about, I will see if he fancies it. It's just that it makes me self-conscious to see all the girls bring their giggly wee friends and the boys bring their pals.

Take Marco Van Keefe for example; a tall blonde handsome smiling bastard, he always has pals with him, and the birds are bonkers for him; his name vibrates in here. Marco sits through in the other main office, and the crazy thing is – in a strange way, we actually kind of look like each other. However, I am the shorter, paler, dark haired, puffier, melted looking version. The symmetry of his chiselled face, or whatever it is that makes him a pure ride, is absent from my genetic make-up – basically, I am the short-arsed mutant discount version of him. So much so, that when I first started in here a pretty girl approached me, and asked, "are *you* Marco Van Keefe?" When I told her that I wasn't, she was clearly relieved. As much as it was a bit awkward and a bit of a kick in the nuts, perhaps I could use him as an inspiration; hammer the cardio, smile all the time like a fucking lunatic, go for sunbeds, put lemon juice in my hair; basically impersonate him like I was a method actor, and hopefully then, get a woman. If only things had panned out better with the band, I wouldn't be sat here like a one eyed, three-legged kennel pooch in desperate need of human contact, or a lethal injection to put me out of my misery, depending on which way you look at it.

The first call comes in, it's from an older sounding lady in Kent. She politely demands to know where I am based as my accent is "so thick." I tell her that I find her accent thick also, and that we will both just have to slow it down and get through the call together, all the while tempted to tell her to take the marbles out of her mouth and ram them up her royal box. Here was me thinking, perhaps naively, that my accent was relatively clear, but I may have to make an extra effort to tone down my burr for the evening as I really cannot be bothered repeating myself time and time again. We get over the whole "I'm struggling to understand you, you're *really* struggling to understand me" bumph and the lady pledges fifty pounds. Yaldy! A big hitter straight out of the gate, I doubt I'll beat that tonight. I thought something like twenty quid would be the highest pledge I would take tonight, but after a frosty start with the whole communication thing, we got there, this auld posh sort really came through for me and set a high bar. I just need to finalise her details on the pledge card and then I am ready to rock and make my line available for more calls. I now want to keep it going, to make up for the fact that I personally am donating the square root of sweet hee-haw.

I'm nearly ready to make my phone available again when I hear from the next work station, "Joe. It is Joe isn't it?" I know that accent. It's HER again. "I take it that was a good call? I heard you say 'woo hoo' after you hung up", she says to me inquisitively. For a moment I can't even talk, temporarily frozen by the complete surprise of encountering her once more. This is getting spooky now, it must be fate – ah, I'll even settle for it being just a series of lovely coincidences. Calmly disregarding my lack of a reply thus far, she continues. "I have not introduced myself properly. My name is Apollina. I came to your house for the book club, but no one was there. Do you remember?" How could I forget? It is seared in my mind. I want to tell her that I remember her wrapped in the light of our garage security lights like some kind of neon-lit super angel, or a Goddess from a distant planet – the most spectacular blur. Clearing the cobwebs from throat I reply, "yeah. Yeah, that's right, the book club." Moving on, as fast as absolute fuck. "What are you doing here Apollina?" She replies, "my friends from university and I saw on the Student Union notice board that the charity was looking for volunteers. So here we are." Just then, Apollina's mobile phone rings. "Oh, excuse me a moment, I better get this."

Apollina takes the call, at first speaking in English, before slipping into French, what I presume is her native tongue – I was right, I thought she was French. French eh? I wonder how long it would take to be proficient in speaking her lingo; to get an edge, to gain that little something extra to help me catch her attention.

Appollina could literally be talking about something as mundane as arranging for the Gas man to come over to read the metre, and such is the potency of her accent, and my complete ignorance of her language, that I cannot help but be utterly entranced. She is the most beautiful woman I have ever seen, or heard, for that matter. Completely oblivious to me, still deep in conversation, I cannot help but just look at her. Then there is that little voice in my head that says, "jeezo, pull yourself together man, you're deep within the Creeper Zone with all of this staring." I give myself a shake and get ready to take my next call. I hear Apollina say "au revoir" to whoever she is on the phone to and I swear, it makes blood run straight to my nudge. Apollina turns to me, opening her mouth to speak, just as my phone starts ringing. I make a subtle "oh well" face to suggest that, while I would much rather continue talking to her, I have to take this call. Apollina smiles in acknowledgement, and then logs on to her phone.

We both continue to take calls, but in-between our phones ringing, there are these little pockets of chit chat between us, and much to my delight, I even manage to make her giggle a few times.

With each soft burst of laughter, more and more it makes me feel like a Goddamn' bazooka wielding fire Viking; she's like some kind of tonic, a human stimulant, a muse in my midst. But this, it is part of my problem; always building girls up to be more than they ever could be. It's not fair on them, and it's not fair on me also – in my head, I build them up to be far more than a mere mortal, I build them up to be some kind of all-loving, all-healing, sex giving super entity. I really must work on this.

As the night goes on and I continue to take more pledges; in the brief moments of silence during calls; like when I am waiting to be told the long credit card number, I immediately drift to thinking about Apollina's name. I mean, as names go, it's really cool. I have never heard it before. It is pretty obvious that it is derived from the Greek God, Apollo, but I am intrigued enough that I will research it fully on the internet. I won't do it just now as, understandably, I don't want Apolina catching a glance of my PC and seeing that I am searching for the meaning of her name – there is every chance that she would freak out and batter me with her handbag.

As the night goes on, the calls begin to come in a little less frequently, which is ample opportunity for us to just bullshit with each other. It's nice, not every sentence is a home run, because it's not intended to be. We're just two people who seem to enjoy chatting to each other; a random comparison – the way I feel just now is similar to when I sat my driving test; I was so incredibly nervous, causing me to make a mistake almost immediately. Presuming that the mistake was severe enough to secure me an automatic fail, and with the best part of an hour's driving still to do, I only continued driving out of personal pride. Thinking that I had nothing to lose, it freed me from my anxiety, my head nonsense. I quickly relaxed, and the rest of the test felt like a breeze, I thought of it as useful experience for when I would inevitably have to re-sit my test. When my hour was up and the driving examiner turned to me and told me that I had passed, I was shocked, but absolutely delighted none the less. And now by comparison, having met Apollina for the first time when my book club failed, and I was squinting and covered in biscuit crumbs, so much of the usual junk and self-destructive brain-farts just didn't seem to be there, discarded by the fact that despite no matter how low I may have felt about everything that first night we met, here we were, chatting comfortably – I'm still breathing, the world didn't swallow me up. Talking to Appolina, all of those usual feelings of nerves, and dread, and awkwardness, were completely absent. I feel like I could just keep chatting to her, no problem at all.

I can see one or two of Apollina's friends logging off their phones and getting their jackets on, before signalling to her that it is time to go. I don't have much time, I know I need to act now. In this moment, there's no stuttering and mumbling causing me to fumble, no nervous energy to blurt out nonsense at a hundred miles an hour, there is just a feeling of calm. It's the state of mind that can only come from being in the company of someone you feel truly comfortable around, I guess.

Apollina reaches for her coat, I quickly switch my phone to Do not Disturb and stand up just a little so that she can see me clearly above the cubical partition. Apollina turns to me and asks, "Joe. Did you really want to start a book club?" She must have sensed somehow that it wasn't a passion project, that it wasn't my number one choice of club. I reply, "no, not really. I am more of a film man, but I had nowhere to host that. My Dad wouldn't appreciate strangers in his living room, and there is no way that he would let me move the TV out into the garage, not even for a couple of hours." Appolina smiles, "well, I prefer films too. If you ever host a film club, be sure to let me know, or even if you wanted to watch something, just with me, I would be happy to." Oh, dear, lord.

"Or, do you think that we could maybe go for a coffee some time?" Did I just say that? This absolute darling has suggested an intimate movie night, and I offer to go for coffee; total friend-zone territory. What is wrong with me? I don't think that she was expecting that reply. Silent, Apollina's initial body language indicates as though it is going to be a case of the ol' polite "thanks, but no thanks, cock-nose." I've never tried the whole puppy dog eyes thing, but this is as good a time as any.

Still, she has not given an answer, she's clearly mulling it over, and if I speak first then there is no chance. But I need to minimise the damage, "look, sorry, of course, we can get together and watch a film. No problem. What I meant, was that we can go for a coffee, as well as taking in a flick together. So that's sorted then; a film one night, and a coffee and a natter some other time as well." Seeking clarification about my local lingo, "a natter?" Clearly confused by my vernacular. "Yeah, a natter, it means to have a chin-wag, you know, just a bit of conversation." It looks as though I may have retrieved the situation, by the skin of my teeth; as Appolina gives me the most delicate of smiles as she reaches for a pen and a piece of paper, quickly scribbling her telephone number on it. "Very well Joe, we shall meet for a movie, a coffee… and a natter", giggling at the use of her newly discovered terminology. By this time, Apollina's friends have already moved away from the bank of desks where they were sitting, and they are gesturing for her to come over and join them. As she walks away with her friends, she looks back and gives me another wee smile, this time accompanied by a small wave. I don't know what the fuck just happened, I don't want to know.

It's a night in with a film and a coffee – some might think, "no big deal", but to me this is huge. No matter, I must try to just let it wash over me. But, the reality is, Apollina is the most beautiful girl I have ever met – the fact that, not only did she not spray mace in my eyes or kick me in the nuts, she actually agreed to meet up with me, for not one, but two, dates, I guess you would call them. This is huge, there are no such things as small victories, right now, anything positive seems massive. Perhaps things are looking up for this wee guy.

The telethon is winding down, everyone is looking at each other to see who of the last men and women standing will make a move first, which will inevitably lead to a stampede of folk heading home or to the pub. Victoria, with her mad unrelenting smiley face pops over, once more invading my personal space, seeking to clarify whether or not I am going to the pub. When I reluctantly reply to Victoria, that I am indeed going to the pub, she enthusiastically replies, "great!" Her energy and enthusiasm for the most mundane of interactions fascinates me, I would die of exhaustion operating at a mere fraction of where she's at.

A group of us make our way out of the call centre, chatting and laughing at some of the more eccentric calls throughout the course of the night, and we head across the street to Hootchy McCoo's pub. It's got a reputation for being a decent enough boozer; good beer and good music, which is all you need really. I have no intentions of staying on late, I have a budget that affords me two to four beers maximum. I am not going to hang around any longer than I can afford, in the hope that people will buy me beers, I may be many things but I am not a beer mootch. Plus, any more than a few beers and matters can get weird, alcohol can spin my mind quicker than that of most casual drinkers I know. Also, depending on how many beers I buy will dictate whether or not I get a munchy for the bus ride home. That's the thing with beers, I can have one or I can have ten, it doesn't matter, regardless it turns my belly into a bottomless pit; I could eat a bin bag's worth of Chinese chicken fried rice. So many times, I have woken up with the gloriously dreadful taste of pakora, donar kebas, curry sauce, and whatever else on my breath, and usually the corresponding stains down my shirt.

The pub is pretty busy, the right balance of having a buzz about it, with all the laughing and chit chat, while not being so busy that you have to wait three millennia at the bar to get served. Plus, an added bonus is that the music is decent, not too much pop charty boy-band arse gravy being blasted in our earholes. A few of the guys from the office ask if we all want to chip in twenty quid each into a kitty, I immediately decline as I don't want them to know how thinly I am treading in my efforts just to be there. I try to own the situation by explaining, "I'll probably only stay for one or two", and when they ask, "are you sure?" I palm them off with, "aye, sure, don't worry about me." Also, I knew that I would look like a bit of a plumb if I were to lay my fourteen quids' worth of coins on the bar, combined they must be about 8lbs in weight – the social perils of raiding your coin jar before a night out.

I buy my first beer, and it goes down an absolute treat, cold but not freezing, nailed it. Such is my enthusiasm, without consciously trying to drink it like a wild man, I have still managed to drink the lot in about five gulps – "Barman, same again please."

Fucking yes – the Cream's "Sunshine of your Love" comes on over the sound system, and I cannot help but put my rock face on a bit. It's just got one of those riffs that puts fire in your belly, a spring in your step, and extra juice in your weapon. It has to be said, that this is turning out to be a cracking night; not only did I meet Apollina, but she, albeit eventually, agreed to meet up with me, and I'm in good company, and there are quality tunes playing. Right here and now, what more could I ask for?

It's fascinating, going for drinks with work folk, I find that people either relax, just let their hair down, and have a laugh about anything other than work, or you get those only shop-talking dildos that want to do nothing more than spew all of their petty grievances and anecdotes of drudgery all over you, completely oblivious to the fact that most people couldn't give a flying fuck, and just want to escape for a few hours. For example; take Big Rosco, until tonight I had no idea what he did out of work – it turns out that he likes to go hill walking, kayaking, cycling, and all this other super fit stuff, but he also likes to go to watch football with his Dad, as well as help him fix up old motorbikes. Big Rosco is quite simply the most interesting person that I have ever met.

Then there is Victoria; bouncing between clusters of people while making work in-jokes, even now, away from the office with everyone chilled out and relaxed, she's "on". It makes my arse ring pucker up. Maybe that's just genuinely who she is at every hour of the day, a fucking mad company-woman. I manage to sneak in a glorious third pint of beer before it's my turn to fall in front of her crosshairs. "Not even treating your boss to a drink then Joe?" Victoria brashly enquires, with her unique brand of alienating unwarranted over-familiarity, and with as much warmth as a frozen fish finger. Boss or no boss, given my budgetary beer restraints she's not stealing my chance to have a final pint, should I want one. I then notice Victoria already has a drink in each hand, which gives me an out. "You seem to be doing alright there for drinks Victoria, I'll buy you one later." I won't buy her one later.

Victoria, in what I suspect is some kind of flirting exercise, feigns offence and replies to me, "alright then, I guess. But I'll hold you to that drink Joe." She then just stands there, staring at me. Victoria hasn't stood still with one person all night before buzzing off to someone else, but it now appears that I am being blessed with some focused one-to-one time. As I look straight ahead, not trying to be completely ignorant, just comfortable in myself with the fact that I have absolutely nothing to say to her. "Great night isn't it?" Victoria says to me, trying to spark some kind of conversation into life. As much as I just want her to leave me be, I'll do my best to be decent and civil, replying, "sure, I was thinking the same thing." Victoria nods with an undeniable, and unnerving, air of self-satisfaction, then slides her bum onto the bar stool next to me, clearly with no intention of moving on to another victim any time soon.

You don't have to be a rocket scientist to work out that she's lined me up for an ear-beating; three-two-one, and there we are. "I mean, it's not just tonight. These past eight weeks or so have just been amazing. A-M-A-Z-I-N-G." She makes me want to rip off my own eyelids and eat them. I find myself occasionally nodding in agreement, zoning in and out, dangerously close to drowning in her swamp of I-me-mine sludge. Christ, having to listen to this shit; put me out of my fucking misery, fatal blow to the brain, wipe me out, make it quick, set me on fire and fling me in the bin.

Victoria, still very much in the zone, continues. "The funny thing is, I've been walking around, carrying this incredible secret."

She's dying for me to ask what the big secret is, but I really don't want to give her the satisfaction, I have never cared less about anything in my entire life. "I know you want to know what it is", Victoria declares, again so epically sure of herself, and that I would care. It is quite astonishing, that in her laser-focus and determination to tell me her news she has failed to recognise, what a blind man could see, that I am being royally freaked out by the sheer intensity of her narcissism. Victoria continues unperturbed, so locked into her determination to dump this pile of bumphery on me. "I have been selected to be the face of the company's entire UK wide marketing campaign – posters, the website, leaflets, I've already shot two TV spots."

Wow, despite my initial cynicism, and general natural feelings of shittyness towards her, that is, undeniably, really big news. I fully understand why she was bursting to tell someone, but why me? I am not tied-in to the gossip mainframe, telling me is a dead end. Regardless, I clink Victoria's glass with my pint glass and tell her, "congratulations. Well done. How did that come about?" Oh, you absolute donkey Joe, damn your fucking politeness, why did you ask her that? What I should have done is congratulate her and then executed a stuntman-precision roll out of the immediate vicinity. Victoria gushes. "Troy from Regional made me aware of this new idea Marketing were banding about, where they would promote an existing employee for their new campaign, rather than hire an actor. So, I applied, went for a few interviews, and I got it. It was that simple really." Victoria just leaves that hanging, I've said my congratulations to her, so what now, what more could I offer her? There is only so much mindless chit-chat that two people who have absolutely nothing in common can muster, surely? I'll just need to play the game, reply with bits and bobs of verbal chutney when prompted, but this can't go on forever.

The longer that Victoria and I are stood here together, the more difficult it will be to break free; with each word, each glance, each giggle, to me, piecing it all together, implies that she is wanting some drunken colleague-on-colleague jungle love action. I could be wrong, but I don't think that I am, Victoria is usually on you, but even she is never *this* friendly. The tension is palpable, but from my point of view it is certainly not sexual, I don't think that I could look less interested if I tried, yet despite these factors Victoria is still fully engaged. Thank the Lord, my tiny child-like bladder kicks in once more and I need to pee, desperately. I find that when I drink beer I average about three pees per pint, it's ridiculous. My weak bladder has always been a hindrance for long car journeys and so on, but not today. After a rare few seconds of silence, Victoria is just about to re-commence with, what I presume is, flirty chat when I say first, "excuse me Victoria, I need to nip to the Gents." Still just smiling at me, like a mad bastard, Victoria smoulders, "okay – hurry back." Fuck me, she is terrifying.

I take longer than I should, but not too long for Victoria to think that I was away taking a dump. Then again, maybe I should torpedo this whole awkward charade, here and now, by telling her that I need to go as I have an ungodly horrific nuclear dose of the skitters. As I walk back to the bar, Victoria is still there. I can see that she is trying to meet my eyes, I don't want instantly pulled back into her tractor-beam, so I try to assess the situation as best I can with my peripherals. I notice that she has her coat on. "It's last orders at the bar, everyone else has left already." Victoria declares gleefully, knowing that there is every chance we could be left to each other if none of the rest of our colleagues are still mulling about outside. Hopefully some of our co-workers are still loitering in the carpark, I grab my jacket and head outside in anticipation of a wing-man to aid me in my escape. Some might say, "oh, just take her round the back and give her a quick drunken rummaging." But I can't, the potential mental-tax would be just too much – sometimes there are people you just can pump.

We leave the pub, and my heart sinks. It is almost as though every single person that we had been drinking with had been sucked into some kind of interdimensional portal; or decided to take a stroll through the sewers, or was air-lifted home via private helicopter, as they are gone, all gone, well gone, not even a dot on the horizon. To the point where I am genuinely baffled as to how they could walk that far away, or all get taxis, in such a short space of time. "So…" Victoria leads with ominously, before coming towards me and, again, way too close for comfort. "It looks as though it's just the two of us", Victoria says to me in a somewhat jarring attempt at a sultry tone, like a cheap sex doll with a wonky voice chip. Victoria moves closer to me, then closer still. I just keep thinking, "all I want is a portion of mixed pakora from the Indian Takeaway and then home to my scratcher."

Victoria has to be able to read my body language; my head lowered and to the side, not making eye contact, arms folded. I may as well be wearing a sandwich board that says, "VICTORIA, GET TO ABSOLUTE FUCK." But no, she goes for it, closing her eyes and leaning in straight in for the kill. My feet stay planted but I instinctually lean back as far as I can to avoid even the slightest lip connection. "I'm sorry Victoria. It's late, and I... I don't think that this is a good idea." Victoria takes a step back, clearly shocked at my lack of reciprocation, rolls her eyes and just stands there, once more, staring at me.

Seconds feels like months. This – is – awkward. But sooner or later, one of us is going to have to talk, one of us will have to break. Fuck it, this shit-show needs mopping up with minimal potential hangover. "I'm sorry Victoria. I just don't think of you that way. I hope that you are alright?" Victoria continues to say nothing, but her expression mutates from a look of shock, to a hell hath no fury-esque rage.

Like I have just looked down at the timer of a ticking bomb, I start to walk away. Starting off slowly, I begin to build up a pace, I walk for about thirty seconds or so and I glance quickly over my shoulder, Victoria hasn't moved. She is just stood there, planted where we spoke, her gaze unflinching. Earlier tonight, I didn't think that she could be any more terrifying, I was wrong.

Luckily for me, I have a week's holiday off from work. It will all die down and everything will go back to normal – rejecting

Victoria's advances is nothing, situations like that happen every day.

We will never talk about this ever again.

CHAPTER 9

Going back to work after a spell of annual leave, there's always that little bit of trepidation; that whiff of paranoia, brought on by not knowing what has gone on in your absence – planting seeds of doubt in your mind, that upon your return, things will not be the same as how you left them. If anything, I should feel lighter, brighter, more rested, because this time, instead of lazing about in my drawers all day, staying up to 4AM watching films, and eating shite, I got up early, went running, ate no take-aways, and didn't have a drop of bevy. I feel better in both body and mind for doing so, plus, I managed to attend an initial meeting with the Citizens Advice Bureau, and they are confident that not only will they be able to put together a debt-busting plan for me, but they will also give me some guidance on how best to generate some savings further on down the line, once my current mess has been attacked and cleaned up.

However, despite my overall outlook being a bit more positive, it doesn't detract from the fact that going back to work this time, there's an added sense of caution; the small matter of inevitably bumping into Victoria at some stage. I don't know if I should be nervous or not, after all; Victoria had had a few drinks, she was in a celebratory mood, and she presumed that I was attracted to her. No big deal. I mean, people have their advances knocked back all the time, it's just one of those things I suppose. I don't feel bad about it, and I am happy just to get the inevitable first awkward "hello" out of the way, and then quickly move on, forgetting all about it. Hopefully, Victoria is cool about it and feels the same way. Besides, she is relocating soon anyway.

The office, usually as warm as a sauna, is cool, and although completely packed with staff at their work stations, there is more of a gentle hum than the usual vibrant buzz of phones ringing and constant chatter. It all seems familiar yet slightly alien; like when you come back to your house after having been away on holiday. "Phones are goosed", says one of the old boys that I catch eyes with as I walk towards my desk. Ah, that explains it, I was beginning to think that I had walked into the most boring lucid dream imaginable.

In rare events such as this, all I can really do is get my desk squared up, check my emails, and be ready for when the phones are back up and operational. I have my supplies for the week; my mints, my sachets of powdered soup, a packet of paper hankies, and a can of deodorant. You always need a can of B.O spray handy, you can't run the risk of dropping a subtle, or not so subtle, "trouser-cough" and not have the means to at least try and cover it up. However, when I go to put my supplies away, my ped is locked. I never lock my ped. I take my key out and it goes into the key hole fine, but it won't turn. I notice a sticker on the side of it, but I didn't put that there. It eventually dawns on me, despite the various clues and clear indicators, that this is not my ped. Janice from my team, pops her head up from her work station. "Hiya Joe. Not your ped? Yeah, a ton of them got mixed up when they were all removed last week when we hosted the telethon." What a complete pain in the arse, that ped was my utility belt; it contained all of my day-to-day survival goods and random paperwork. Hopefully, it will be returned soon enough – I don't think that there is anything in there that I should be worried about; no contraband springs to mind. It's just that my ped is the only thing in here that I have attached any sense of ownership to, and while not the end of the world, I would really like it back sooner rather than later. Everything else around my desk; it's just paper, folders, and plastics; AKA shite that can go in the bin.

Still, there seems to be something more in the air than the mass annoyance caused by a few peds getting misplaced, the feeling; vibe, whatever you want to call it, it feels off. Unable to let it lie, I seek assurance, and info, from Janice. "Janice, everything alright? Seems a strange atmosphere in here today." Janice is always good for info, as and when required. Very relaxed, she informs me, "everything has pretty much been the norm – no scandal or any real news to tell you about." Great, that is such a relief to hear, as my paranoia was starting to grow arms and legs there, brought on by my concerns that "news" of my rejecting Victoria had become common knowledge, resulting in word-of-mouth muck flinging PR disaster, spreading faster than the speed of light via the office-gossip network, and that I was now on the Bastard List.

However, my sense of relief was misguided as Janice was not done. Janice continued, "although, I don't know what her problem was, but Victoria's face was like fizz; I mean she was a right old vinegar-tits all last week. But, whatever it was that was bothering her, she must be over it now, as I bumped into her this morning and she was back to her bubbly self." Oh dear. Shit. I'm not sure how to feel about this. Hopefully, and most probably, it has nothing to do with me, at all. I am sure that our little post-beers knock-back situation was not the cause of her torn face last week, surely?

I begin to go through my emails. In these rare occasions when the phones are down there is very little else you can actually do. Each email is just a fluff piece, nothing really of note; internal comings and goings, kittens for sale, such and such got married, thingymajig retired, the usual kind of stuff that nosey folk are drawn to, and that the rest of us acknowledge briefly in the most basic cognitive way possible, before dissolving in the dark recesses of our brains, never to be retrieved again. There must be nearly a thousand people working in here, I am lucky if I know a dozen of them, and the folk I know don't tend to pop up in the emails. "Phones are back on in two minutes guys", a Floor Manager shouts across the office. Good stuff; I was beginning to get a bit bored there, running out of things to look at – all of the football websites are blocked by the I.T guys, which is especially frustrating just now; as there is a strong rumour doing the rounds that Celtic are trying to sign Matin Minelez, the Croatian born target-man with the Brazilian father, apparently one of the best natural finishers around.

I give it a couple of minutes before I log on to the system, immediately my first call comes in. I instinctively put my hand out to lift up my phone, when someone else's hand comes across mine in a blocking motion. It's Victoria. "Don't pick that up. Log off. Come with me", Victoria says to me coldly, ice cold.

As I begin to follow Victoria, she makes sure to stay a couple of feet ahead of me at all times, at no point looking back at me. As we move through doors and corridors to parts of the building that I do not have security clearance for, Victoria just keeps scanning us through, door after door, corridor after corridor, all the while remaining completely silent. What a fucking oddball. I mean, everyone, no matter who they are, or who they think they are, has had to deal with, what my pals and I at school used to call a KB; a knock-back, by someone at one stage in their life. I thought that it builds character to be rejected, that it's part and parcel of the terrifying terrain of looking for a mate – I didn't lead Victoria on, in fact, I attempted to keep her at arms' length during every single interaction we ever had. I was not playing it mean to keep her keen, I wanted her, at all times, to fuck right off. I am now beginning to think that I should have just kissed her and avoided this peculiar scenario, but who knows, that could have added yet another perilous dimension to this gumph.

We have been walking for so long, that eventually we arrive at a series of offices that I didn't even know existed, way deep down within the bowels of the building. Finally Victoria decides to communicate with me again, turning to me and nodding her head in the direction of a door that I presume I have to go in. I open the door to see Mr Flanagan, Regional Human Resources Manager for the North of England and Scotland, sat at his desk, which has nothing on it apart from some plain paper. All I keep thinking to myself is, "what the hell is this about?" Mr Flanagan is tall, I estimate around 6'5 at least, with dark smokey grey hair; a looming figure that oozes dusty crusty awful dullness. Dullard or not, he has a reputation for always going by the book and, when required, being a bit of a quiet assassin in the firing stakes. Mr Flanagan opens in his monotone voice, "take a seat please, Joseph." "Joseph?" No one has called me that since I was six years old, and as small a factor as that is, this most basic lick of formality is enough to start the alarm bells ringing in my head, and get my arse-piece squeaking.

Victoria takes a seat next to Mr Flanagan, directly across from me. At first, Victoria looks like the cat that got the cream, all smugly satisfied and with a face that you wouldn't get tired of skelping with a giant rotten trout. But as the seconds pass by, more and more, she is slipping back into "crazy face", the very same expression that was on her face the night she tried to kiss me. Sat there, 12 o'clock from her, I am being frazzled like a fried egg in the heat of her odd, unsettling gaze. Mr Flanagan pipes up, "I imagine you are wondering what this is all about, Joseph." No shit, you grey aura laden bastard. I say nothing, it was clearly a rhetorical question, but nonetheless I give the smallest of nods in acknowledgement, doing my very best to remain a blank canvas, rather than openly display my true feelings; that I am completely bricking it. Mr Flanagan continues, "As you are in no doubt aware, there are a lot of changes taking place within the organisation." Oh, fuck off! Spare me the clichéd you're-about-to-take-it-up-the-arse-corporate-scene-setting bollocks and get to the fucking point. Flanagan continues, "...and with such changes, it means that some members of staff will be moving onward and upwards to new and exciting opportunities, such as Victoria here. However, those members of staff whose positions have remained rigid within the organisation, well, it is my responsibility to assess their contribution and tighten this area of the workforce, as and where I see fit. Which I am sure you understand?" Again, he can fuck right off, but once more, all I can offer is a silly little nod. You don't need to be a member of MENSA to know what this rocket means by "tighten" –

it's corporate prick speak for sending people to the dole que as the result of a number crunching exercise.

Flanagan takes his glasses off, clearly for effect. Jesus, he thinks he's a detective in some US cop drama. "So, Joseph, it is with this in mind that I need to shine a spotlight on those not quite pulling their weight; monitor them, coach them, give them the adequate support, but if required, terminate their employment." Where the FUCK did this come from? Why am I even in a room with this nob? Now in full flow, Flanagan puts his glasses back on as he says to me, "and that is why I have asked all of my Team Leaders to identify those within their respective teams, those who would perhaps benefit form a little motivational chat; to refocus their efforts, and get them back on-side." Oh dear, the corporate wank-chat just keeps on coming, spewing out of every pore of his big pasty unit – this man's years in some HR dungeon may very well have stripped him of any form of original means of expression. Flanagan continues, "…and unfortunately, it has been brought to my attention by Victoria here, that you, Joseph, *you* are a person of concern. A case illustrated by your monthly appraisals." Wait, hold on, what? There must be some mistake. My monthly appraisal reports were always positive, and signed off with a couple of comments; along the lines of "targets met/exceeded", and to "keep it up."

While I am just trying to piece it all together and make *some* sense of this, simply too stunned to speak, Flanagan overturns the sheet of paper in front of him and delivers his hammer blow. "This document here, Joseph, is formal written confirmation that you are being placed on the Competency Scheme – a six week long assessment period, whereby depending on your performance, it will dictate whether you retain your employment with this organisation, or not. Do you understand everything that I have just gone over?" Oh I know what it means alright, it means that I am being rail-rolled out of my job, you dick! In response I muster a strange exhaling noise, something along the lines of "nhyuh."

I glance over at Victoria, she is LOVING this. The sense of satisfaction, brought on by her swift retribution, is bursting out of her; it is clear that Victoria believes she is fully justified in her actions, in so much as, she believes that I have wronged her, and as a result, I must be punished severely. It is almost too much for her to contain, but she keeps it subdued enough to remain undetected to Flanagan. Flanagan closes the meeting by informing me, "that's all for now, Joseph. Victoria will escort you back to your work station", before looking away, completely disengaging eye contact, such is his apparent disdain. To him, I am just another number to be crunched; just another ingredient in the big bowl of shit soup, that is his job.

Victoria opens the door and I follow her out. Again, scanning us through a series of doors as we make our way towards the main office area, and still, she does not look back at me, not once. I'm completely scunnered, the sense of injustice is frying my brain. It's too much, I stop dead in my tracks, before the final security door, and finally decide to call Victoria out on her bullshit. "Victoria. What the hell is this all about?" Victoria whips around to face me, clearly astonished that I have the sheer audacity to question her, as she snaps, "excuse me, how dare you?" I don't want to make this any worse; in this moment, I know that no matter what, I have to remain cool. In the hope of reason, I keep my voice low and even-keeled. "Victoria, look, this is insane. You know that my reviews were positive, all of them. I've never had a single problem here, so I don't know what the hell you've told Flanagan." My mind is racing, then it dawns on me. "I get it now. You didn't even show him the reviews, did you? Flanagan is putting me through this, based purely on your say-so, isn't he?" Victoria, so utterly sure of her convictions, slowly walks up to me, leaning right in, only a couple of inches from my face, looks me dead in the eye, and whispers – "oh, I have copies of the reviews, don't worry about that, and the reviews don't lie. Facts are facts, Joseph". Victoria completely avoids answering my questions, not to mention my pleas for reason. What's the point? Of course, Flanagan is going to trust Victoria, she's the company's golden girl now – to doubt her would be company-politics suicide.

I really, *really*, don't want to go there. But sod it, needs must. Still, somehow remaining cool, I continue. "Look Victoria, we both know what this is all about." Victoria's smug smile drops instantly, turning to pure rage. I continue regardless. "Victoria, that night, after the telethon, in the pub car park, you feel that I have hurt you in some way; led you on, gave you the wrong signals. But that's not how it was. You have to put a stop to this, right now. My livelihood is on the line here." Victoria, still visibly fizzing, pauses – I suspect to regenerate and sharpen her tongue. Having had a second to get back into character, the look of pure anger subsides and *that* fucking smile washes over her again, accompanied by that condescending tone of hers. "Joe. Joe, Joe, Joe. I'm up with the big hitters now. There is nothing, NOTHING, the likes of you could ever do to knock me out of my stride, and if you know what's good for you, you'll never mention *that* night, ever, again."

Victoria walks away from me, scanning the final security door that leads us back into the main office area where my work station is. I follow her until I am clear of the security door, I then stand for a moment just to watch her as she continues on; mingling, shmoozing, shmoltzing; making small talk with colleagues as she passes by, smiling and laughing – as if absolutely nothing had just happened, as if her reservoir of ire had not just made matters a whole lot worse for me than they ever had to be. What a horrible human being. What a complete and utter fucking monster.

CHAPTER 10

What a long shitty day. I am sat in the smokers' shelter at the rear exit of my office, by the car park. It reeks in here, but I don't want to sit about my office, and I cannot bring myself to get on the bus during rush hour, not tonight.

There must be some way of getting through to Victoria, but what can I do? Nothing, there is nothing I can do. I have zero recourse; the reason being, and not everybody knows this, as I can't even remember how I know this, but Victoria was married, then divorced, at a very young age. During this understandably fraught and difficult time, Victoria formed a strong lady-bond with Liz, who coincidentally was also going through a divorce around the same time, resulting in them becoming each other's "besties." What has this got to do with anything? Liz is the HR Manager for this site; she has an entire team working under her, and she is a person of great influence around here. Liz and Victoria are tighter than a snare drum, and to make matters worse, Flanagan has a deep professional appreciation for them both. On the face of it, to all of the major players concerned, I am not deemed worthy of the steam off their pee-pee.

I am feeling like a bit of a darling, but surely what is good and right and fair should prevail? There must be some kind of platform to enable me to make my case; find an ear willing to listen, or just someone who can look at the facts – I have never received a negative monthly appraisal in here, ever. To have Flanagan cut my legs off, purely on Victoria's word, or have my appraisals doctored, as I suspect Victoria has done, just because of her inability to handle the most minor of rejections, is beyond comprehension. I mean, it's fucking unbelievable!

But, there *should* be copies of my monthly appraisals. Oh shit! Fuck! That's it! If I had my copies of my monthly appraisals, it would completely vindicate me. Appraisal forms are like receipt books, in that each sheet has two parts; once Victoria and I would go over my appraisals, we would each sign it to say that we both agreed with what had been discussed, and that I was satisfied with the accuracy of Victoria's notes. The procedure is that Team Leaders keep the top copy and staff would keep the secondary blue copy.

But, most probably, I probably threw them in the bin, or in the best case scenario; *maybe*, I scrunched them up and put them in my ped, amongst the rest of the junk and random discarded bumph. However, with the peds having all been jumbled up on the night of the telethon, and there being around a thousand desks in here, I would have to search them all, just to have even the faintest chance of providing evidence that supported my claims. Without them? No chance. If I were to try and put my case to Liz with zero evidence to back me up; she would be sure to reject it out of hand, inform Victoria of my tattling, and subsequently any prospect of me retaining this job would surely take a nose-dive and head straight down the shitter. I have no doubts; it would be a kangaroo court; totally pointless, merely a human experiment in maintaining the crumbs of the little integrity I have left. I can't even go off on the sick, they would see that a mile away. To do that, I may as well curl up, admit defeat, and resign. But I *need* this job, there are so few around, and even fewer for young drop-outs with not much experience of anything.

I am sick of this, *fucking* sick of it for that matter. Sick of always being beholden; under some weight that I can't shift; whether it's lack of conviction and confidence to pursue my musical passions alone, regardless of whether or not the boys ever wanted to join me, or my lack of qualifications, or my credit card debt, or Victoria and this shitey job. It's been over a year now, I am tired of clawing at the mirage of validation; striving with all my might for the inner knowing that I am, or ever will be, enough. Am I to be just another zoomer, warped so young that I cannot see a time or place where I won't have this chip in my shoulder, or be drawn to pre-determined misery and, at the very least, discontentment? I have been let out into the big bad world and it is eating my hairy bollocks for breakfast.

CHAPTER 11

Lying on top of my bed, still fully clothed. I haven't even taken my shoes or jacket off; the most basic standards of behaviour slipping away under this cloud of panic and confusion. What am I going to do? When the boys and I had our falling out it was because I didn't see the signs; I was too blinkered, too deeply entrenched in only what I wanted, so completely unable to see the wood for the trees. But with this, I have full clarity on the matter, I have done absolutely nothing wrong. It feels like a higher power, if one even exists, knows that I am down and is testing me; sensing my vulnerability, it's poking me in the eyes and twisting my nips.

I didn't want to kiss Victoria, it is that simple. There was absolutely no point; I am not, and never have been, attracted to her. I have always thought of her as barely tolerable, and even still, in very small doses; given that we have nothing in common and she appears to have as much depth as a concrete filled garden pond. I could completely understand if there was an initial awkwardness between us, or she kept a lower profile out of feeling a tad embarrassed, or anything along those lines. But to manipulate matters so that I could lose my job, it just stands as testament to the pathetic fragility of her ego. Ever since I started this job I have felt so terribly miscast, and I hoped that one day I would leave, but on *my* terms, for bigger and better things. As dreadful as I have always considered my job to be, I now find myself clinging on, tooth and nail, to keep it.

In my head, I just keep thinking things like; "Victoria, what a fucking bitch", "or imagine her doing that to me, the evil cow." It changes all the time; "tart", "slag", "witch." However, the more that these negative thoughts swirl around my head, it gets me thinking – if I were ever to say these things aloud, people would perhaps think, given my anger and my use of words, that this was specifically an anti-women thing. But this isn't an anti-woman thing; if a guy was doing to me, what Victoria is doing to me, I'd be calling him; "prick", "bastard", "arsehole", and the likes. My internal fury is aimed at a horrible person, regardless of her gender. I keep thinking about this, as I don't want to teeter anywhere near the edge of becoming bitter and twisted towards women, just because one of them has been especially horrible to me, after all, I would eventually like to find love and settle down with one, one day. I am trying my best to formulate opinions about people on an individual basis, and discard some of my more immature and narrow opinions – I reckon I will live to be over one hundred years old, and on my death bed, I'll "get it." A life spent learning, just how not to be a tosser.

This stress man! I can't bear the thought of just sitting around the house, but I can't bring myself to go for a jog either. Sat here huffing and puffing, I am beginning to annoy myself, I'll meet myself somewhere in the middle and opt once more to vedge on the park bench on the hill.

I sit down on the bench, this place is becoming my temple of solace. I begin to take in slow, deep breaths; in then out, in then out. I just need to keep doing this, in the hope of clearing my head and fire-fighting the anxiety that is consuming me.

It's useless though, no matter how much I try to regulate my breathing and get my thoughts in order, I can't. The same question just keeps ringing in my head – "why is Victoria doing this to me?" My job was the one aspect of my life that I thought I was managing well. Sure, it was monotonous shite, but I got there on time; I hit my numbers, and while my interactions with my colleagues were never spectacular, they were at the very least, civil. I never saw myself being there long term, I always thought of it as a steady income until I made my next move, whatever that may be. To have this one aspect of positivity stripped from my life because of one daft, egomaniacal, toxic, bastard, it's just so bewildering. At least when the band split up and I made a tit of myself, it was pretty much self-sabotage, but Victoria throwing me under the bus like this is a completely different animal all together.

"Not running tonight son?" Jesus! He's done me, again! "Walter, you scared the hell out of me. You're like some kind of OAP ninja". Walter stands to the side of me with a huge grin on his face, clearly proud as punch at giving me a fright once more. Walter continues as he takes a seat. "Aye, I've still got it, auld twinkle toes, that's me." Walter takes a moment to sit down and get comfortable, sitting back, nose raised to soak in the evening air.

Eventually, Walter chimes in with, "nice night. Isn't it?" Not especially in the mood for small-talk, I reply, "Yeah. I guess it is." More silence follows, the kind of silence between two people that makes you suspect that when one of you does eventually speak again, the conversation could go absolutely anywhere.

"Son. I hope that you don't mind me asking, but where are your pals?" Jesus, Walter has not so much addressed "the elephant in the room", but climbed on top of the elephant, kitted it out in a party hat and disco lights, before making it charge straight at me with a hard-on. Walter continues, "a nice enough lad like yourself shouldn't be sauntering around all the time on their own." Walter getting *real* with me catches me off-guard, leaving me bamboozled, providing a unique combination of emotions; a crushing sense of embarrassment and awkwardness, brought on by someone I barely know putting me on the spot and making me stare down the barrel of something that I would much rather avoid.

I am not going to break down and cry, but there is undoubtedly this emotionally-driven grinding to a halt of my physical being; like at any point I may vomit up a spanner or a broken part. I take a moment to get it together, in the hope of replying in a calm and measured manner, hoping to not give too much away. However, despite my intentions, all my guts come spilling out. "Walter, I guess you could say that I'm not exactly where I want to be right now; I still live at home with my folks, my friends and I had this massive falling out, and my job has gone to shit. That's why I often feel like just sitting around on this bench and staring into space like a total queerhawk." Walter bows his head and nods in acknowledgement. "Mmhm. I'm sorry to hear that son", Walter replies sincerely. As then continues, "where are your family in all of this?" Here goes, the full download. "Dad and I don't have much in common and Mum doesn't say much. I have an older brother called

Andrew, he's the real success story; he's an environmental lawyer, but he moved away. Sitting in my house, three strangers wandering about like ghosts, I'd rather just sit out here and watch the world go by." Walter doesn't seem too impressed, his face hardening ever so slightly as he replies. "Never take your parents for granted son, they're the best pals you'll ever have in this world, and they won't be around forever." It would appear that I have touched a nerve, I've most likely pissed him off, but perhaps he should sit in our living room while my Dad swears at the snooker on TV and my Mum sits in the corner smoking her menthol cigarettes, barely talking, letting out the odd acidic, sneaky, tiny-smoker-person farts, and see if he doesn't become complacent in his admiration for the sanctity of parenthood. Or maybe I am just being a nasty wee prick?

I get the sense that Walter is the determined type, not one to let things go un-straightened out. Walter continues, "you don't have much in common with your Mammy and your Daddy, and your brother has moved away. But what happened with your pals?" For a moment, I think, "hold on here, I don't know this old codger, I don't owe him anything. Why should I explain myself to him? It's none of his business." And then this calming, yet sad realisation kicks in, that at least there is someone willing to just sit down with me and have a chat about my problems. I am in no position to be pushing any more people away – this unholy union of self-destruction and misfortune must come undone at some point.

Once again, deep breathes, as I poise myself. "We had, eh, we had a falling out. And now they're gone, they're on the other side of the world. There are a few guys that I know from the local pub who I could get in with, if I wanted to, but they're into different stuff from me." I am hoping that Walter doesn't dig too deep into the "different stuff" that I am referring to; he doesn't need to hear about my perception that, almost overnight, cocaine seemed to spread from Glasgow and the other big cities and land in the suburbs like an atomic bomb. Thus, the more sociable aspect of drinking was now hindered by young men and women, thinking they were cute, rebellious, and interesting, sneaking off to do lines of coke in piss-soaked toilet cubicles. Again, fucking again, I am not part of the clique, I am on the outside looking in, a voyeur of shared experience. It would have been whisky and ale in Walter's day, not the "Columbian marching powder."

Walter takes his hat off and turns to me. "I'm sorry to hear that Joe. Maybe you and your pals could sort things out. Everyone needs pals, and those who says otherwise are just kidding themselves on. It is never easy when the people you care about move away, I know all too well. I have a son, his name is Stewart, he moved to America nearly twenty years ago; speaks with an American accent, he calls curtains "drapes", and taps "faucets'", has the accent, the full shooting match. When his American friends say his name, they pronounce it Stoo-art instead of Stew-art like we say it. I get to see him around once a year, if I am lucky. He's an engineer, he could work anywhere he wanted, the world's his oyster." Walter stares ahead, it's abundantly clear that he misses his boy, because as brief as our encounters have been, it's the first time that I have seen his spirits dip, if even only for the briefest of moments.

Although, he must have given himself a shake, not wishing to ponder on his absent son any longer, as he quickly changes gear; re-sets himself, smiles, and then puts an offer to me. "Anyways, I was thinking. This Saturday my social club are going on a trip to Glasgow. We're going to the Kelvingrove Museum and the Transport Museum, and you young Joe, are more than welcome to come and join us?" Eh, could I go? I mean, I've never hung about with a squad of old people before. What if they are a pain in the arse, or one of them dies, or does something completely mental that

I am not expecting? I have to seek some sort of clarification. "No offence Walter, but will I not be the only, you know, young person there?" Walter laughs like I have said the most ridiculous thing in the world, before replying. "Maybe. But in all seriousness, there are people of all ages who tag along for these trips; friends, family members, they're a good bunch, you'll like them. Oh, and it's free. Old Tam, the daft bugger, went over his ankle playing frisbee with his Grandson, so he has to sit this one out. The bus, your lunch, it's all paid for, so you don't need to worry about any of that, and it would be a shame if the place went to waste." Do you know what? Bollocks to it, what have I got to lose? I'm going to do it, I'm going to befriend the elderly. "Walter, I'm in." And on that, we shake on it.

CHAPTER 12

Saturday morning arrives, Walter told me to be at the Community Centre for 09:30 – it's 09:40 and I am still a couple of minutes away. Briskly walking, I realise that I will need to up the pace and start running if I am to have any chance of catching the bus, such was my under-estimation of how long it would take to get there.

If they have waited on me, at this rate I'll be sweating like a rapist by the time I get on the bus – I am hoping that I am sat by a window and that I can hang my head out of it like a wee dog, to help cool me down. Luckily, they have waited on me. Standing by the passenger door of the minibus is Walter, shouting towards me, "move your arse Joe." All flustered, I make my way over. Typical, the guy getting to tag along on a freebie, holding everyone up.

Out of puff, I quickly make my apologies, to which Walter dryly dismisses, "aye, just hurry up and sit down." The doors of the bus close, the driver starts the engine, and Walter introduces me. "Everyone, this is Joe. Joe, this is everyone." In unison, the rest of the passengers on board reply, "hi Joe." I quickly take a window seat near the front, beads of sweat dripping down my brow, and with that, the driver releases the hand-break and the bus starts moving, Walter, as proud and commanding as the Captain of some grand old ship, declares, "and we're off", and in reply, we all let out a mighty cheer.

In only a matter of minutes, a simply astonishing array of hard boiled sweets, mints, and chocolates are passed throughout the bus. There is enough to choke a big fat donkey, so much so, that by the time we exit the Clyde Tunnel I feel a bit peaky due to the sheer intake of quality munchies, especially with it being so early in the morning.

We arrive in Glasgow's west end and the driver parks the minibus, and like a herd of cats, we make our way into the Transport Museum in dribs and drabs. Immediately, as we enter, right by the front door, are two old cars; a BMW Isetta and an Austin Mini mk1. Walter beams, "oh look at that! I had an Austin just like that you know. My father-in-law gave me his when his health took a turn for the worst and he became too poorly to drive any more. Oh my, isn't she a beauty." To the left of the Austin Mini mk1 is a replica cobbled street, lined with old fashioned shops, giving young bucks like me a glance into the past; they have an old pawn broker, a dress fitting shop and a really old toy shop, not to mention the old-fashioned mens' pub, where women were only allowed in to collect beer for their husbands. I had forgotten all about this place, I haven't been here in years – looking at all the shop windows, you really do get a sense of how things were back in the old days, long before I was born.

This sense of exploring the past is deepened when I see the prices for the products in the windows listed in old money; a farthing, ha'penny, thrupenny bit, sixpence, shilling, two bob bit, half crown, and ten bob note. It is safe to say that despite multiple attempts by various people to explain to me what any of these terms of currency mean in relation to modern money, I still don't have a scooby. Among the shops on the replica street there is also a Picture House – it fires my imagination to think about all of the people, of all ages, coming to see news reels and double features, as no one had TVs back then, with not a "regional accent" to be heard; all of the news narrated by some posh bloke speaking in the Queen's English.

For a moment, I wonder what it would be like to turn up at a Picture Hall in Glasgow in, for example; in the 1930s, and screen a modern big budget, action packed, Sci-fi movie, with all of the incredible special effects that modern films can offer, and just sit back and watch as it blew everyone in the audience's mind. You would probably have folk fainting, crying, jumping out of windows, and so on, over something we are now conditioned to, and that we take for granted. I don't know why, but I always day dream about silly scenarios like that.

I don't quite know what the smell in this place is. It's not a bad smell, I presume it's a combination of all the old leather interiors, the oil from the engines, plus the paint from when they touch up the artefacts from time to time. The aroma is a shade stronger than subtle, and it accompanies you wherever you go in here; whether you are looking in and around the old cars or steam trains, busses, trams, motorbikes, or bicycles, as soon as that scent hits your nostrils, it is like a silver bullet of nostalgia to the brain.

All this time, I remind myself that even though I am there as Walter's guest, I should be careful not to smother him and be too clingy. I try my best to hang loose and mingle amongst his crowd, and such is the size of the museum, our party constantly splinters off in various directions, only to periodically reconnect throughout the morning, so it is easy to come and go as I please without looking like a random phantom straggler.

Approaching lunch time, eventually, everyone gathers together as we make our way across Argyle Street to the Kelvingrove Museum. The weather is surprisingly nice; it's bright with not too many clouds in the sky, with only the faintest breeze blowing every now and then. The squad I am with seem delighted with the weather – the subject of the weather is a classic ice-breaker and staple of everyday chit-chat, especially with these mad old tarts. Ordinarily, I am not really one to talk in any great depth about the weather, but these old folk do, they really do, they fucking love it.

After the obligatory check for dog shit, like a hippy commune we all sit down on a nice spot of grass on the grounds at the Argyle Street side of the museum. One of the ladies opens up a large cool-bag type thing and starts handing out sandwiches. "Eat as much as you want", and "there's more than enough to go about" is the message, so it would be rude not to get tore right in. Jesus, these pieces are magic. "Tea or coffee Joe?" Asks a nice older gentleman. Having been introduced to people in fits and starts throughout the morning, it dawns on me that everyone seems to know my name, but I have been unable to retain any of theirs. I have always been terrible with remembering names; like mathematics, my brain does not naturally retain such data. I reply to the nice man, "I'll have a tea thanks. My apologies, what's your name again?" My inability to remember his name does not seem to have bothered him a jot, when he calmly re-informs me, "I'm Frank." Frank, Frank, Frank, you need to remember he's called Frank, Frank is a good guy and not a wank. Frank, Frank, Frank, not a wank, guy's called Frank. Right, got it, the nice old guy who gave me a cup of tea is called Frank (and he is 100%, carved in stone, not a wank). Hopefully later on if I speak to him again I don't make a Freudian slip and just blurt out "wank" to his face, but I'm sure I'll be fine.

This is like being at your aunties; cracking grub, cups of tea from the Gods, and now there's chocolate biscuits getting dished out; good ones, no snidey cheap ones or outright duffers. There is plenty of nattering and laughing, everyone seems to be having a whale of a time. This is magic; nice weather (acknowledged internally), an amazing picnic, the people could not be more warm and welcoming. I want more of this; simple pleasures, with good company.

I just want to take it all in – I lie back for a moment with my hands behind my head, and I close my eyes. This is the most relaxed that I have felt in ages; the sensation like a slab of concrete has been laid on my chest is gone, I remember to just breathe, breathe slowly, breathe deeply. "Oh, looks like someone has had too much lunch and wants to go for a kip. Come on fatso, we're only at the half way point." I open my eyes to see Walter standing over me, offering me a hand up.

We make our way into Kelvingrove Museum. It's a beautiful big building, I always remember the local legend that the architect who designed it committed suicide because it was built the wrong way round. But apparently that is incorrect; the grand entrance was always meant to face the River Kelvin and not Argyle Street, as most people would presume. Had the architect done himself in over this, I could understand; if I make a mistake with the most basics of tasks; like I forget to put the bin out, or I select the wrong setting on the dishwasher in our kitchen, it makes me want to shoot myself, never mind making a boo-boo on the scale of getting my angles wrong in the construction of a grand old building.

Again, I could not tell you the last time that I was here, I think it was probably a school trip when I was around thirteen years old or somewhere around that age. As soon as we make it into the main hall, just as we had earlier in the morning, everyone splits up into groups of twos and threes and goes their own way. With so much to see, in such a large building, it was bound to happen.

I like looking at all the stuffed exotic animals; there is a tiger that has paws bigger than my head, and if I ever had the misfortune of meeting this big glorious cat bastard in the wild he would eye me up like I was a turkey drumstick, I would not stand a chance. Then I look at the replica dinosaur bones, and I don't even want to think too much about what those bad boys could do. Based on fossil findings, they have put together the skeleton of a Velociraptor; the claws, the teeth, a truly terrifying proposition, it's no wonder that it took a planet threatening meteor impact to kill those dirty big beasties. In the description below it, it says, "a bird-like Dinosaur of the Mesozoic Era", well if that's the case then the Mesozoic Era can braid my arse hair and piss right off. When time travel becomes a thing, I'll go back as far as Woodstock to see Jimmy Hendrix and leave it at that, I'll leave the bird-lizard-monsters to their own devices.

I go up the stairs for a look at the painting galleries. As I walk around, I can't help but think that – with art, any kind of art; whether it's a poem, a song, a film, a book, or a painting, it really boils down to one thing – you either get it or you don't. I mean, I walk around here and I find most of the stuff quite interesting, but I reckon that if I had more knowledge about the historical context about these paintings; about the people, the places depicted, and those who put paint to canvas, I would like, and appreciate, all of this even more. *Or*, I could become so knowledgeable that I would be able to critique all of the exhibits to the point where I found work, I had previously thought was nice to look at, now to be shabby and "not to one's taste", now that I could cast my gaze upon them with my educated eye. But as things stand, I am wandering through the grand corridors of this place safely in my own little bubble of gleeful ignorance.

As I continue to breeze from one gallery to the next, I have no idea as to where I am going. Eventually, I turn a corner and there is Walter. "Hi Walter, what are you looking at?" Standing in awe, Walter replies to my question with a question of his own. "Have you never seen this before son?" I am not entirely sure. I reply, safe in the knowledge that he'll probably think me a classless shlub, "erm, ah, I think so. Actually, I don't know." Still, locked in sheer admiration, Walter cannot look away. "This is Christ of Saint John of the Cross by Salvador Dali. It's a masterpiece." There is no denying it, it is an impressive painting. Having been born into a practising Catholic family, the only angle that I had ever previously seen Jesus on the cross was straight on; frail, beaten, broken, nails through his hands and/or wrists. This was the first time that I had seen a depiction of Christ's crucifixion from a different perspective; with no blood, no visible nails in his hands, no crown of thorns. I don't know what an art critic might say about it, but to me it's kind of dizzying, because when I look at it I cannot figure out if Jesus is up in up in space, or he's in heaven, or if he is only a few feet above the ground. I have no clue as to what the figure in the bottom left, or the boat at the harbour, represent. And although the water is calm, the clouds in the sky look ominous to me. But not to Walter, he sees the picture in a different light completely. "Just look at it Joe. Jesus, God's only son, made the ultimate sacrifice, he gave his life so that we could be free from sin, all of us. To see him here, dying on the cross before the world, and the sun just about to peer through the clouds, it tells us…" Walter pauses, as if the swell of emotion might just be too much for him. Before continuing, "it tells us that although our Lord is dying, he will rise again to shed his light upon the world, and deliver us all from evil. I love this painting."

Old school; having suddenly become aware of his open display of vulnerability, Walter self corrects, breaking from his gaze to check his watch. "Oh my, look at the time, I can't be late." Walter says before hastily walking away and going around the corner. What the hell is he late for? No one mentioned anything happening that was timebound. I look over the balcony and see, one by one, our party gathering in the main hall of the museum. I decide to head down to see what is cracking. As I get down the stairs, the gang see me, they usher me over with raised whispers, "quick, hurry, you don't want to miss it." Miss what? Then at that moment, the giant organ, that looms magnificent over the main hall, starts to play, it's Walter! Up there, as cool as you like, he begins to play the Procol Harum song, "A Whiter Shade of Pale." The sheer might of the organ's sound fills the entire museum – so melodic, so flawless. So much so, that I feel my eyes begin to get a bit sweaty, oh deary deary me, get it together man. But it's pretty damn powerful, and undeniably, more than a little touching.

Walter, fair play to you old boy, up there like an absolute pimp, not a nerve in his body. When the song ends the gang begin to clap, but I can't help it, completely caught up I belt out, "yaas Walter, get in there!" More than a few puzzled expressions are aimed my way, but as short a time as I have known Walter, I can safely say that I was very impressed by the whole thing, and for what it's worth, I would go as far to say, I was proud of him.

The group and I stand around chatting, everyone is absolutely beaming. After a couple of minutes Walter appears, I cannot hide my enthusiasm. "Check you, ya old dark horse." Walter smiles at me as he pats me on the shoulder, "no bother son, no bother." It's nice when someone can surprise you like that; show you another facet of their personality, take me for example; I can talk pish, and I can talk shite too. One of the ladies remarks to Walter, "such a pit that your Rose has the flu, she would have loved to have seen that." Walter, ever the gent, simply nods in acknowledgement.

The bus driver appears at the museum main door, he tells us that the parking meter is up in ten minutes and that we need to be making tracks. Walter's jaunt on the grand organ, which sounds a bit homo-erotic, was the perfect way to finish a day that went a thousand times better than I thought it would, or ever could, have gone.

We all get on the bus and make our way back home. Out of the goodness of his heart, instead of dropping everyone off back at the Community Centre, the driver drops off everyone at their homes or at the very least, near to their homes. As the day has gone by, I have picked up peoples' names; Jill, Jill's on the pill; John, John with a big red face like a strawberry bon-bon; Anne, Anne loves fake tan; Doreen, Doreen drinks chlorine; Arthur, Arthur has a smelly farter. I remember their names in my own, *very* childish, way. But at least I'll not forget them now.

As each person steps off the bus we all say "cheerio", and a fair few of them very kindly thank me for coming along, which is was very nice of them. Each time, I reply sincerely, "thank you, it was *my* pleasure." Without question, it is I who should be thanking them; for the free day out, the free lunch, but most of all, for the company. But not only that, they were good company, no, better still – they were great company. If you could bottle up the kindness, warmth, and sincerity that I was shown today, I'd drink it by the gallon. There is no question about it, had you proposed this day to me a year or two ago, I would have made my excuses and avoided it like the plague. But having given it a go due to my current social life being more than a bit sparse, I can say with the fullest of my heart that this is the best day I have had in a long, long time.

CHAPTER 13

The posty was early today. I caught him just before I set off for the day – more scary letters arrived for me; that horrible bright red font, words like; "urgent", "important", and "do not ignore" emblazoned underneath the address box. The snake is tightening its grip, I'm breathing unnerving short breaths, the concrete weight on my chest is back, and it feels heavier and heavier with each letter that arrives through my door. I am worried that the weight is too heavy, that sooner rather than later, I won't be able to catch my breath, and there will be nothing left for me to do but fall. All of this; the debt, my job, pining for my mates. I am spinning all these plates – plates of shit.

Gathering myself enough to get out of the house and on my way, there is at least a crumb of rest bite. Every now and then, my job requires me to attend mandatory training. Most of the time it means spending a half-day in one of the on-site conference rooms. However, sometimes you get lucky and are sent up to Glasgow, to the company training centre in Finnieston. I have to admit, I am surprised that the company are allowing me to go; when I first received an email notification about this particular training day, I was certain that Victoria would kibosh it, thus enabling her to keep her crazy beady eyes on me.

I am glad to get at least one day away from all the bullshit that is going on back at the office, and *perhaps* the fact that I have been permitted to attend this training, it means that there may be hope for me yet of retaining my job. Surely, they wouldn't waste their money on training someone that they are just about to can – or – perhaps it is just standard policy to ensure that while you are still on the books, you are not discriminated against?

Today, the course is called "Diversity in the Workplace." This could be a winner, because I would like to meet and befriend people a bit more exotic than myself; I am white as fuck, and everyone I know is white as fuck. It would be nice to add some flavour into my life; learn some foreign patter, eat their Granny's exotic food, be seen out and about as a racially sound character. My Grandparents were all Irish, but most of the people I know come from the similar backgrounds, so I have no racial or cultural ace up my sleeve, we are all white and Scots/Irish as fuck together. A boy I used to know went to Thailand, and he said that over there, there were people who used certain products to make their skin lighter, but over here everyone wants to be darker – we all want to be gorgeous tanned bastards. Perhaps, that if darker skinned people want to be white, and vice versa, then it just goes to show that most people fundamentally do not like how they look. Maybe after this course today I will gain a better understanding of why we should just treat everyone as a beautifully crafted individual, with their own unique story to tell. Still, would be nice to have some spicier friends to show off.

I make my way towards the training centre, and just as I walk across the pedestrian crossing at the slip road onto the Clydeside Expressway, I notice that someone has graffitied on the pavement – "I miss how I feel about God." Just reading this, as criminally naff as it sounds; it stops me dead in my tracks. How strange, how strangely profound, it might not register with many folk that walk past it, but it certainly strikes a chord with me. You see, I think about this quite a lot, having abandoned my faith completely. But it's not only that that catches my eye; the font and paint of the graffiti; the white paint is so clear and bright and neat, the complete opposite of what you would ordinarily associate with graffiti randomly crudely etched on a pavement, like; "Big Shug Luvs Wee Maggie", or "fuck the polis."

I wish I believed in God, I really do; the ubiquitous cloak of strength and comfort that comes with having a faith, providing answers, raising you up from the depths of despair – what a blissful aspiration. But I don't buy it.

Every week, for the first seventeen years or so of my life, I attended mass on a Sunday morning with my family. As I was born into it, I never knew any differently. I looked forward every week to seeing my friends and relatives, but I always considered the act of attending church to be just another routine task; like making your bed or brushing your teeth; you have to put your nice trousers on and go to mass once a week. Although, the chocolate egg at Easter and the sweets at Christmas were undeniable annual highlights.

After I made my First Holy Communion, I remember that it was nice to finally get the opportunity to wait in the big que to receive the sacrament by eating the wafer. But I was never too keen on drinking the wine, purely out of life long concerns relating to oral hygiene and the mental imagery that comes with the term, "drink the blood of Christ." I would eat the wafer, more often than not, it was the first thing that I had eaten that morning as we would always be running late and not had enough time to eat breakfast. The wafer would tend to get stuck on the roof of my mouth and I would be paranoid that I looked like a dog eating peanut butter, as I made my way back to my pew to pray. Eventually, I would be able to retrieve the wafer, however the second that I swallowed it my empty stomach would always begin to make loud rumbling noises. Kneeling down, eyes closed, I would make a real go at praying; I would wish for the best for my family, and that the moany teachers at school would cut me some slack, and that in general, I would be alright. But the older I got, I would tend to just day dream; there in the darkness of my closed eyes, the smell of wood polish from the pews and the incense in the air, there was complete disconnection; I had grown tired of projecting good intentions into the abyss.

As the years went by, I started to formulate my own ideas, and I developed my own questions – I had begun to pick apart something that I had always been taught was infallible. I stopped going to church, and it felt weird. I had gone to mass every Sunday my entire life, but the less you go, the less compelled you feel to go.

But there is still an internal nagging sometimes; that perhaps I am missing something, that perhaps if I spoke to the right person, I could rekindle or develop my faith. For example; there was a guy that started in work at the same time as me, his name was Pierce. Although, he quickly moved on, as I think he went back to give college another go, he and I would car share as he lived not far from me. Pierce was a devout Christian, and he was more than happy to talk about his faith. However, I never found much depth to what he had to say; I would ask him lots of questions; basically, I was looking to hear his opinions on the aspects that I was not entirely comfortable with, in an attempt to have an adult conversation while trying my best not to offend him, as I didn't want it to look like I was trying to wind him up just for the sake of it, plus, he was a very intense character. But all he kept saying to me, each time with more and more gusto, regardless of the question, was "God gave his only son for us. Jesus died for us." It was as though this blanket statement should more than adequately answer any of my queries or concerns. But I thought that for Pierce to keep replying to my questions again and again with the same response was a complete copout – surely it can't be that simple; God has hundreds of millions of followers because he gave his only son to free us from sin, Mrs McCluskey who lives round the corner gave her only son a year ago, to what most are now calling an illegal war, and no one seems to give two shits about her. Often, having not gotten much out of Pierce, perplexed, I would eventually settle to just sit in resigned silence, with Pierce happy that I had finally shut the fuck up. I am not for one moment saying that all Christians are like Pierce, but he has been the only person interested in chatting to me about it, most people I encounter don't tend to adhere to any religious affiliation these days.

However, in the quieter moments of my day, I would still think about this stuff. Then, in a sub-conscious nervous panicky moment late one Saturday night, having not gone to church in months, I felt as though, to allay this curiosity, I had to go at least one last time and find out once and for all if it still had its hooks in me. The next morning, I got up and went to church. I stood near the back and the mass began. This peculiar sense of guilt washed over me; that I was somehow an imposter for even being there, and because of my evaluation of the proceedings, now that I was detached and looking at it more objectively. For the most part, it seemed archaic and strange, and I might go as far as to say that in some parts I found it silly, cruel, and hopeless. But more than anything, it served to confirm that this lamb had well and truly left the flock.

A key component of my life that had always been there, was now gone; that community, that shared experience, the sense of ritual, and in many ways, a certain sense of identity. It is a shame that the families that I grew up with, I won't see them every week now; new born babies in their parents' arms growing up to be wee cheeky monsters, and the funerals of the nice older folks one by one moving on up (or down) to whatever lies beyond. There are one or two aspects that I will always have a fondness for; like when the Priest says, "we will now offer the sign of peace", and everyone shakes hands with those around them and says, "peace be with you." Such a simple, yet powerful gesture. Then there is the prayer for the deceased - "Eternal rest grant to him, O Lord; and let light perpetual shine upon him." No one knows what awaits us when we die, but no matter the incarnation or dimension we find ourselves in, I do hope that if there is the possibility of eternity in the dark, we find ourselves basking in the light.

However, certain factors would always pop into my head and often supersede any nostalgic fondness I may have; like when right before partaking in the Eucharist, the congregation prays aloud in unison, "Lord, I am not worthy to receive you, but only say the word and I shall be healed." I know that I am a mere mortal and all that, but to willingly declare aloud that you are not worthy? I mean, when you take a moment and just think about that – people are born into the faith of their family, that wasn't their choice, and indoctrinated into this mantra of utter worthlessness. It's disgusting. No wonder so many people are completely fucked up by self-loathing, guilt, and confusion.

Then there are all of the other factors; while I was never abused, and to my knowledge none of my friends were, the institution, all the way up to the very top, is complicit in the covering up of decades long, maybe even centuries long, mass child rape on a global scale. I mean, that alone should have caused the whole thing to come crashing down.

But what if I compartmentalise it; and for a moment, I separate the powers that be from the congregation, and think about it in terms of; what if by making every-day people live, or want to live, a good life or help their community, and whether or not it is real or some kind of spiritual placebo, the mere fact that it motivates people to be nicer to each other should supersede some of my complaints, and that I shouldn't tar it all so blindly with the same brush. It's not black and white, and neither is how I feel about it. It's hard to shake it off completely.

I will probably bounce these ideas and questions about my head forever; why aren't there female clergy yet? What is their problem with the gays? Why are clergy to be celibate? It all strikes me as man-made bullshit dogma, and indicative of the lesser qualities of mankind; fear, guilt, repression, and cruelty, all of which combining to shape policy. The cool Jesus that we are taught about; hanging about with the whores, thieves, and cripples, I don't think that he would give two hoots about consensual adults fulfilling their sexual destiny – but some nasty, sexually confused, shame riddled man or woman most likely would.

But then I think about how Walter spoke about God, that time when I found him in awe of Dali's painting in the Kelvingrove Art Gallery. I once read somewhere that there are no atheists in fox-holes; as when in the unique conditions of war, with death looming ever present, everyone makes a pact with God; that they will serve him for as long as they shall live, in exchange for safe passage out of whatever living hell they find themselves in. I imagine that many of those that got to come home from war, having made that pact, and having witnessed what they did, the gratitude of God would be firmly in their hearts.

I am just a young man, I know pretty much fuck all. If all of this brings people comfort and helps to guide them in living a loving, peaceful life, then who am I to argue? I am just some wee guy, a complete loser, stopped in his tracks by graffiti, most probably written by some zoomer who had drank too much tonic wine and was feeling a tad philosophical. I just want to go for a sleep.

CHAPTER 14

I haven't been sleeping well at all. Although, I did have a lovely dream about Apollina last night – not too racey, it was simple really. I was lying on my back in some imaginary room, Apollina leaning her face over mine, gravity causing her hair to cascade over me; cocooned in her long brown locks, her sweet smell filling my brain, her slowly and gently peppering me with soft kisses from her gorgeous full lips. It might not be as weird and obscure as me flying about the place, but this is better.

But my dream, as sweet as it was, was still part of a night's sleep that overall, was still very much disturbed. As strange as it sounds, there is only one sure-fire way I know of to secure some quality zzz's, and that is going to see a film. I suspect that this comes from a childhood spent dozing off in front of the TV; watching films on old beaten up VHS tapes. It is not uncommon for me to fall asleep at the pictures, only to be awoken by the sound of people leaving their seats as the end credits role. Bizarrely, I should probably look into investing in a cinema seat for my house, to nap on.

I often wear my hoody when I go to see a film, there in the dark, cut off from the world, that is my optimum comfort zone. I don't usually have any money to buy soft drinks and popcorn, which is a pity because if I could afford it, I would eat a bin bag full of salted popcorn and still want more, regardless of the salt level madness. While I can rarely afford snacks, and despite the nuclear shit mountain that is my finances, I still have not surrendered my monthly cinema subscription. For £13.99 per month I get to see as many films as I like, I used to be more picky, but now I will watch any old pish.

Fancying a right good kip, I take the bus to my local theatre. As I walk in, I put my hood up, in the off chance that someone I know sees me – I would rather just breeze in and out without having to make awkward small talk. As I approach the ticket counter to flash my monthly membership pass, I glance at the film listings on the electronic display screen on the wall, none of the film titles jump out at me, so I choose the one that is starting the soonest. Heading to my screen, as I drift through the groups of friends, families, and couples gathered in the foyer; waiting for their film to start or for other people to arrive, getting their snacks, and chatting away – I feel like a ghost. This just highlights my constant inner conflict; I put my hood up not to be seen, but deep down, deep deep down, I would like to find a familiar friendly face and have a laugh, no matter how much I try to kid myself otherwise. There is this seed of hope in me; a certain knowing, that this is just a chapter, and I just need to ride it out for as long as it takes, and that I'll be back here sooner than I know, with a girlfriend, or some pals, and when I do I'll really appreciate it. Just now, to survive I just need to keep deluding myself that this lone wolf shit is for me.

The film starts – it's an American court drama about a high-profile politician who has been wrongly accused of killing his wife. It starts well enough, a decent film to stumble across. It stars some guy I am sure I have seen before in the role of the lawyer, and some classically beautiful posh looking sort as his hot lawyer sauce companion. I presume that there is sexual tension as the story develops, but it's clear that this film is not a game changer; it's a paint by numbers, you could watch it with your Mum, type film. Not that there is anything wrong with that, there is comfort in the steady hum of the frequency of mediocrity. Now the guy, the lawyer guy, he seems like his confidence is all front and perhaps the case is too big for him. The posh sort, she's all front too, but she wants to see the lawyer guy really shine before she jumps his bones, and both of them are being threatened because there's more to this case than meets the eye, and... I don't really care.

This hoody that I am wearing – when I die, I want buried in it. It is the provider of the most comfort that any item of clothing has ever brought me. This cinema seat, it doesn't disappoint – as I am sat there it feels like it is cupping my chunky wee arse cheeks, almost as though it was custom made. I surrender my back muscles to the embrace of the cushioned upholstery, the psychosomatic nostalgic bliss chemicals flood my brain. And like that, I am out for the count.

As is tradition, the credits role just as I wake up. As naps go, that was glorious. I give myself a minute to recombobulate. There's no rush, no one else is sat in my row. I could strip bollock naked and do cartwheels if I wanted to, as very quickly I am the only person left in the entire screening.

With the last of the credits rolling, I do something that I would never usually do, I look at my phone. I have always believed that there is a special place in Satan's ring-piece for selfish bell-ends that look at their phone in movie theatres, but as I am the only one here, I permit myself this time. A text, but not just any text, it's a text from Apollina, you absolute dancer! It reads, "Hello Joe. Meet soon? A x." Yes! Yes-yes-yes. I feel that charge, that inexplicable zap to the system, of when someone you have the serious hots for shows even the most basic interest in you. It's mad to think that only four simple words in a text from Apollina could raise my spirits so much; I want to go for a jog, lift some weights, hack down some trees, do a dance, slap an arse. I don't care about coming across as too keen, this is the time for action, so I reply immediately. "Yeah. Sounds great. Say, this Saturday afternoon at the Bean Corner coffee shop? We can plan our movie night."

Now, I wait, like a fiend. But who am I kidding? I should worry about coming across as too keen, because now any form of distraction will be welcome, as I will undoubtedly obsess over when Apollina will reply to me, and what she will say. You see it all the time, when people have it together and their life is fully stocked with friends, families, associates, activities, and events, interactions such as this come and go. But not me, not where I am at. Such are the gaps in my life, that when someone, or something, comes along; that nervous energy, that over eagerness, it takes hold and I pounce on it like a dog with two dicks and I fixate on it, obsess over it, and ultimately threaten to jeopardise it before it even has a chance to begin, suffocating all potential in its inception. But the over eagerness is nothing new, it has crept up on me at various points of my life, people seem to pick up on it straight away, and I only recognise it miles down the road. The times where I have failed to get a handle on it, before my very eyes I can see it unnerve those that I am trying to connect with, such is the reek of social anxiety and desperation. Although, the text message I just sent aside, perhaps I could learn to chill the fuck out and gain the discipline required to just relax and take it easy.

The message I need to get into my thick skull is "no more texts to Apollina until she texts me back." Like an exorcism, I need to cast out the creepy obsessive instinct, and not *try* and chill out, but actually succeed in chilling out. Perhaps if I did overcome this nonsense, Apollina would continue to warm to me, after all, she has agreed to meet me – maybe if I kept it together, she could be my muse, be my co-pilot on my future adventures, leaving all this bumph far behind.

I stand up and make my way out of my screening. Having given myself a bit of a talking to, I feel good, like there's a glow around me. Apollina texting me makes me feel like I could burst into dance or start throwing karate shapes; like crazy kicks, somersaults (although, I am not sure that has anything to do with karate), and verbal outbursts of "wooo chaaa" and "ha-yaaaa." Jesus, I am damn near strutting like an old skool pimp.

As I make my way past the other screens that lead back to the foyer, I put my hood down as I am smiling and I no longer feel like hiding. I usually have to go for a quick pee when I come out of the pictures, but my mind is elsewhere, I am absolutely buzzing that Appolina is seeking to meet up. "Joe. It is you. Joe." I turn around, and standing right there, it's Donald. Shit.

I am not ready. I am not ready for this. I try to speak but a strange mousy squeak is all I can muster as I attempt to reply. Donald looks at me with bitter sweet eyes, like I am an old broken toy that he found in his loft; something that he has a kind of nostalgic fondness for, but that isn't part of his life anymore.

Both stood in silence, forced to bask in the awkwardness of this being our first encounter since I made a rip-roaring tit of myself on the night of our big gig. The other issue is, that it was my understanding that he and the other boys were off on the other side of the world – I *really* did not expect, nor want to, bump in to Donald like this. I am just so taken aback, I wish I could snap into full mojo, but I can't. I then notice Donald's little brother, Brendan, is standing a few feet away, glued to his mobile phone as he thumbs away at the buttons, dressed in a tracksuit, his t-shirt spilling out the sides, completely oblivious to the tension in the air, and all round uncomfortability.

Had it been just another ordinary night at the pictures that I bumped into Donald, then I *might* have been better prepared mentally to face him, but having been on such a high after Apollina text-messaged me, it's just too jarring, too much of a bump back to reality. It soon becomes clear that my silence will not be stood for; Donald, such a laid-back cat ordinarily, leans towards me, clearly agitated. "You're just going to stand there and not say anything, like a fucking oddball?" Despite Donald's anger, Brendan does not divert his gaze from his phone. I manage to find my voice, just enough to eventually muster a reply, "it's been a long time, I thought you were still away.." But I am unable to finish my sentence as Donald interjects, "I'm just back for a funeral, my Gran died. You should have replied to our emails." He is that angry, that for a split-second I think that there is a distinct possibility that he is going to gub me one right in the moosh, and the two of us are going to end up rolling around on the floor. Donald gathers himself; changes tact, lowers his tone. "Look. Joe. I know that things got out of hand that night of the gig, it was all just a big misunderstanding, and I know that it wasn't easy for you. We should have nipped this in the bud the morning after, sorted everything out, and you should be out with us instead of being back here all alone and bitter, licking your wounds."

It hurts like an absolute bastard, but he's right. But it's all too far gone, I'm too far gone, they've had all this time together without me; travelling all over the world, making new memories, basking in new experiences – and I've become a fucking husk creature.

Again, I am taking too long to reply as I try to think; the tumble and swirl of my mind overloading me, the words just not coming out. I'm just standing here not saying anything. With a look of disgust, like I am shite on his shoe, Donald brings our impromptu meeting to an end. "All this time Joe and you still can't shake it off. I'll leave you to it. Brendan, come on, let's go." Brendan, without looking up from his phone, instinctually follows Donald like an obedient dog. They walk away, under my breath I say, "don't go", but such is the determined pace that Donald is walking at, he is too far away and doesn't hear me. And like that, they were gone.

I guess that no one likes it when the people they are hiding from find them where they would least care to be found. That's me, that's now. And I didn't even have the presence of thought to pass on my condolences when Donald told me his and Brendan's Granny had died.

The boys aren't going to keep emailing me forever, they probably never will again after tonight's debacle, and I am astounded that they have done so up until this point. I know that the offers of an olive branch are finite. Once again, what a complete tadger I am.

I make my way through the empty foyer, leaving from the opposite side of the building from where Donald and Brendan left. As I make my way outside, the cold night air bites my neck, I put my hood up and make my way to the bus stop. The night air is making my eyes moisten... the night air... the cold night air.

CHAPTER 15

Yet another day at work out of the way; totally spaced out, phoning it in. I haven't even been home yet, I couldn't care if my folks find any dodgy debt letters, fuck it. Sat on the bench, again, staring into space, again, underneath this big fucking looming tree, again. I am wondering if Donald is still here or if he has gone back to meet up with the boys yet. After the other night, is there any way he would entertain me? What would I say? Perhaps there is a chance that we could patch things up; that we could scrub that collective memory and start afresh, move on, be *sound* again.

Christ, how I miss them all. If I could just find it within myself to apologise for being such a twonk. But the reality is, it's not that simple; even if I had the balls to try and patch things up, I still have this debt around my neck. To walk away from it and leave someone else to clean up my mess, or stay here and work out a way to pay it off, neither are a short-term solution.

"There you are." Walter declares. I genuinely think that this old mad man has taken about six months off my life, at least, with all of these sneak attack conversation starters. "I've not seen you since our trip", he informs me very matter of fact, before continuing, "the committee's trying to organise another jaunt. I'll put your name down if you're interested?" I will definitely go, for the amazing sandwiches alone. "Sure, Walter, I don't see why not", I reply, trying to pretend that our trip to the museums wasn't the most fun I had had in ages. Walter grins assuringly, safe in the knowledge that he could tell that I had a great time on our first trip, and that I am trying to play it all down.

"Anyways, what is new with you young Joe?' Walter asks me, clearly keen for a chinwag. It's safe to say that I won't be sharing my story about bumping into Donald, however I will be more than happy to tell Walter about my coffee date with Appolina. "Well, you know, just the small matter of meeting a girl for coffee." Walter silently makes a "whoo" expression, before chiming in, "a girl eh? I hadn't fully abandoned the idea that you might be a wee gay guy. Good for you! Best of luck with that." I can't help but laugh, it's touching to see this news get Walter so intrigued and giddy. "Well, like I say son, I am happy for you. I'm a romantic at heart me, oh yes, always have been."

"Rose and I started courting six months before I went off to war. Along with Mother, I could barely bring myself to leave them behind. Rose asked me if I thought that we should get married before I go, but as much as I loved her, I didn't want her to be a young widow should I not return home – the future, everything, was too uncertain. So I promised her that I would do my best to come back in one piece and when I did we would get married and settle down.

There were times during the war when I'd be lying back trying to get some sleep, in some strange foreign land, and despite everything else going on around me, Rose was always on my mind. Sometimes I used to wonder if it would be better if I could just forget about her, but the harder I tried, the more she was there, always at the forefront of my thoughts; I would wonder if she was safe, and how she was getting on. Thinking of her gave me something to look forward to, that despite all the madness, rubble, blood, and loss – there was still someone who could bring me light.

When the war ended, I was stationed in France. Before my conscription I had never even been out of Scotland, and by the time the war was done I had fought in numerous countries, on three different continents, and could speak four languages fluently. Not too shabby for a wee boy from the Gorbals. I knew that soon I would return home, and when I did I would make Rose my bride.

I still remember it like it was yesterday. In my final days of combat, I burned the palm of my right hand quite badly, I could never forget this, because as soon as I arrived back in Scotland I went straight down to surprise Rose at the church where she volunteered. Such was the pain in my right hand, still heavily bandaged, I had to bless myself with my left hand when I entered the church. What a setting; despite having sustained some damage in a German air raid, overall the church looked splendid, and there by the alter was Rose – now a few years older than when I saw her last, she was more beautiful than I had remembered. I paused for a moment to compose myself, Rose completely unaware of my presence as she and the other volunteers placed candles by the alter.

I was ready, I could not wait a moment longer. 'Rosie!' She turned, dropped an unlit candle that she was holding and ran down the aisle towards me, I opened my arms and she jumped on me.

I had never felt anything like that in my life; her legs wrapped around my waist, I spun her around, my head buried in her hair, inhaling her scent. Rose pulled her head back to look at my face, with tears of joy in her eyes she said to me, 'I can't believe you're home.' I put my forehead to hers and whispered, 'neither can I my dear, neither can I.'"

Oh for fuck sake, my eyes are welling up. Oh Walter, you old git, I am a right soppy tart at times, especially feeling as vulnerable as I am. That, that there is just a nice story, there's just no getting away from it. But I cannot show Walter that his story has got me all emotional, he already breaks my balls enough; I let out a strange throat clearing coughy type noise, readjust myself, keep my emotions in check. "Walter, eh, that's some, that's some story." Quietly satisfied, Walter replies, "thanks son. That's us been married fifty seven years and I love her now more than ever." I can't help but say to Walter, "you're a very lucky man Walter." He turns to me, and warmly replies, "never a truer word spoken my boy."

Walter stands up, declaring, "I better be off. By the way, don't worry, I'll be sure to put your name down for the next day trip." He knew that I would want to go. "Thanks Walter, just let me know when, and how much, and I'll square you up." Walter replies assuringly, "I certainly will." And as he goes to leave, he pauses for a moment to say, "oh, before I forget, good luck meeting that girl. Just be yourself, and you'll be fine." Pearls, the old boy's giving me pearls. "Thanks Walter, see you soon."

I hope I can come back to Walter with a success story. What he is saying isn't rocket science, but it is easier in theory than in reality.

CHAPTER 16

It goes without saying, but war terrifies me. Hearing Walter talking about how he was away fighting, for years, during World War II, it is mind boggling. The war "we" are in right now seems like a totally different animal in comparison. Back when Walter was at war, the mission was clear. But this, this seems like a bit of a muddle, an illegal muddle at that, and a lot of people seem to be dying in the process.

If the conflicts in Iraq and Afghanistan keep ramping up, it has crossed my mind that the government might bring back conscription. Given my shitty eye sight, I would be no use in combat, I would have to sit it out and just hang around locally, trying to pump the lonely military wives, doing my bit for the cause.

As things stand, more and more troops are heading over as part of the "war on terror". Although, a lot of people are asking what Iraq has got to do with any of this, and what the connection is between them and what happened on 9/11. To me, it's madness, it's like punching your dentist in retaliation for the botched job your mechanic did on your car, there is no correlation.

I don't know where this will all go, and how much it will cost, but none of it looks good; the civilian death toll over there must be unspeakable.

It is a year since 9/11. I am not sure that the world, or at least us living in the West's perception of the world, will ever be the same again. I wasn't alive when JFK was assassinated, until 9/11 that was the ultimate "where were you when" question in sitting rooms, bars, and offices, all over the world. In terms of big news days, I remember the space shuttle, Challenger, blowing up, and growing up the IRA were rarely off the nightly news; to this day, I will never understand the ridiculous decision to overdub Sinn Féin Leader, Gerry Adams, whenever they showed footage of him speaking. Even as a kid, I thought that was fucking stupid, and insulting to the public.

But 9/11 was the first time that I was glued to the TV, bearing witness to a truly historic and influential event, and the most high-profile act of terrorism, probably ever. I will never forget it, I was watching "The Phantom Menace" on that Tuesday afternoon, and trying desperately to like it. Subdued, as the end credits rolled, I pressed the stop button on the remote control for the VCR, and the TV defaulted to a terrestrial news channel. I could see a sky scraper on fire, I had not been able to work out where this was taking place, when at that moment, the second plane hit. It was then that the newscaster speculated with some confidence that it must be a terrorist attack.

That day, as news of the other hijacked planes came to light, the Pentagon being hit, the other plane going down near Pennsylvania, and the days and weeks that followed, I remained in front of the TV, everyone seemed to be.

I had heard of the World Trade Center, but I had no knowledge of what it looked like or how it dominated the Manhattan skyline. I knew what the Empire State Building looked like, but I have never been to New York, I have only been to America once, we went to Orlando when I was five years old and I remember very little of it, other than it was bright and hotter than hell.

Many people I know, most of whom have never been to New York also, now have framed photos or canvases of the Twin Towers in their homes, as though they were compelled to show solidarity with the people of New York, and commemorate the fallen and their families.

Some people have speculated that 9/11 was an inside job. I'm not sure about that, but the world seems to be a crazy place, so

I guess anything is possible. What I know for certain, is that things haven't been the same since, and we are an ocean away. It felt like the façade of safety had been wiped away, and that all the bombs and attacks that you would see on the news from time to time on the other side of the world, that might as well have been a million miles away, had the distinct possibility of landing on our doorstep.

It is unlikely that anything will happen in Scotland, seeing as all the war mongering is decided in Westminster. What am I talking about? We have all the nuclear subs up here and secret hollowed out military mountains, of course we are a target. Yeah, we're all fucked.

CHAPTER 17

Apollina and I agree to meet for a coffee at 3pm. I was secretly pleased at this, as it's a kind of an betweeny time and hopefully it nullifies any expectation that she may have that we should go halfers, or God forbid I have to pay for the lot; whether it be a late lunch or an early dinner. A coffee and a muffin each is about as far as I can stretch, and it would be a stretch. I know that it's a shitty way to be thinking, how I wish things were different. It's not nice, it's not good at all.

I arrive at the coffee place at 2:45pm, I want to make sure that we have a decent table and that I can ease myself into the room – I cannot be sat sweating like a nervous zoomer, too warm or just plain anxious at not being able to secure a decent table, or a table at all.

Luckily the café is a nice moderate temperature; when places are too warm it stresses me out as I just get so uncomfortable; crazy warm bloodedness has always been a root in much of my anxiety. Apollina arrives, she's early too, it's 2.55pm. I like this, none of that fashionably late, too cool for school, bullshit. I go to stand up and Appolina gestures for me to stay seated as she makes her way to the counter – "what would you like Joe?" Here was me with all my preconceptions that I would have to pay for everything – newsflash dickhead – there are no rules, just people. It just goes to show, every day, life is teaching me lessons; it's not the 1950s, I shouldn't be so focused on what is expected, as it's such out-of-date old bollocks.

Back to the task at hand – what would I like to drink? I can't just say a coffee, it *has* to be something a bit sexier – "a mocha please." Yeah, that'll do it, she'll think that I'm a guy with a sophisticated coffee palate and not some kind of simpleton who opts for just coffee with milk and one sugar. Besides, does anyone actually like coffee? I have always thought of it as tasting like a hot chocolate that has gone off, and it makes you have to take wicked dumps like an absolute champion. Here's hoping this mocha does not blow the bunghole clean off me, I can't be trying to make a love connection, surrounded by arse musk.

Apollina is asked by the barista what she would like, to which she replies, "one mocca... and a white coffee please." Again, I am wrong, again, instead of just being myself, ordering what I wanted, and not trying to overthink things, I pull from my caldron of nonsense the notion that my choice of drink would have any bearing, at all, on anything. It is times like these, where it makes me think that in my developing years, I should have spent more time in the company of people, and less time in front of the TV.

Before moving away from the counter, Apollina asks me, with a big smile on her face, "would you like a cake, or a panini, or something?" Wooft, this is some kind of next-level madness, bringing grub into the equation. I ate some cereal about 90 minutes ago, I don't want to eat something and have it squat in my stomach like a stray cat – "I'm ok thanks, I'm just great...thanks." Whoo – check me – I expressed my true feelings and sounded almost like a normy there.

The barista quickly makes our drinks and Appolina places them down on our table as she says to me, "there you are Joe, enjoy." I am such a sucker in her presence, it's tragic; her most basic interactions, how comfortable she is in her own skin, it's all so effortless. She radiates this breezy, warm, friendly aura; just pure loveliness. I know I am getting carried away, I am undoubtedly a bit of a crawler, but I cannot help it, Apollina is just smashing.

We start to make light chit chat, and before I know it, time is flying by and we both seem to be enjoying ourselves. In the brief comfortable pauses between conversations, I am abundantly aware that my esteem for Apollina continues to grow and grow; she is just so alive, and present, and warm, and calm, and it's just really nice to be in her company, even if it's just for a coffee (or should I say a mocha, that is absolutely honking). But I don't mind.

When asked about myself, I give very little away, instead I try my best to direct the vast majority of the conversation back towards Apollina, in a very general sense, as to not come across as too focused on the detail, and ultimately a bit too nosey.

People who arrived after us are already leaving, but there we are, still nattering away. Appolina begins to tell me about a guy called Bruce from her university class that really annoys her and when she says, "he is what you might call, a wanker", I nearly die laughing. So much so, that Apollina starts to laugh like crazy also, it's great when laughter becomes contagious like that, like a self-fuelling fire. In the midst of our laughing fit, Apollina warms me no end when she says, "Joe, I like laughing with you."

Apollina's laughing finally climbs down, resting at a hearty smile, and just then, I get this sinking feeling. It's like I am being dishonest; like I am trying to sell her a bad bill of goods. I can't keep papering over the cracks, it is wrong for me to even try. For example; my aunt Linda, she was always a really decent soul, but she married some absolute arsehole with a ton of baggage – he clipped her wings when she should have soared through life. I'm not going to be the kind of person that does nothing but take, and drag folk down.

My face must be a right picture. "Joe, is everything alright?" Apollina asks me, before enquiring further. "You were laughing so hard and now you look so serious." I take a moment, before I let it all out, to let the black sludge inside of me have its day – "Apollina, this was a mistake, I shouldn't have met you today." Apollina lets out a nervous giggle, "what do you mean Joe?" My jaw clenches, as it's one thing to always think it, but to say it out loud, especially to someone you just met, is something else altogether. "Apollina. Look, you're the coolest, smartest, and most beautiful person that I have ever met in my life. Me? I'm just a fuck-up." Confused, Apollina repeats, "a fuck-up?"

I'm on a roll here, best to power on. "Yeah, a fuck-up. I blindly pursued my dream of making it in a band with my pals; oblivious to all the surrounding factors, I gave everything I had, in every sense, but none of in panned out. I wasn't smart about any of it; I got myself into debt, neglected my education, ruining any foundation I had of being able to make any head-way in life in my twenties, and worst of all, I blamed it all on the people I cared about the most in the world. So here I am; lonely, in debt, and I am just about to be rail-rolled out of my job by some maniac, all because I wouldn't give her a kiss one night down at the pub, that same night that you and I sat next to each other at the charity telethon. All of this could have been avoided if I looked around me, listened, you know? I could have combined band practice with some studying, given myself some options, not been so gung-ho with the credit cards. But this is where I am at, and oh, how could I forget, I still live at home with my parents who look at me like I am a one eyed, three legged cat. So, as stated, I'm a fuck-up."

Astonished at the swift change of mood, and my making matters super weird as the result of me recklessly spewing my guts out to her, understandably, Apollina asks me, "Joe, why are you telling me all this?" I look her straight in the eyes. "Apollina, it's because I like you. I really like you. And, I'm not sure if you would ever be interested in me in that way, but I don't want to be dead wood for anyone. I just need to work off my debt, get focused on getting a job that I can hold down, then hopefully get into college, then, when I have a sense of control, some direction, then I might have something to offer." Awaiting Apollina's reply, I think please don't start with "I'm sorry to hear that". Apollina slowly reaches over and places the palm of her hand on top of mine – "I'm sorry to hear that, Joe." Oh shit. Apollina continues, "you clearly have a lot on your mind. Take some time for yourself, but not too much. As bad as you believe things to be just now, they will get better." I bow my head, that old familiar feeling of sweeping resignation.

Poor girl. What did she ever do to deserve me unloading all my baggage on her like that? Apollina, she doesn't even know me. My actions; the selfishness, the sheer galling narcissism – fuck me, it's astonishing, it's relentless.

Apollina stands up and puts her coat on. "Joe, nothing is determined. You can change this, all of it." Apollina walks away, I stare straight ahead, but using my peripheral vison I see that she is nearing the door. I can't help but look towards her, she glances back at me with a kind of deflated, "oh well" expression. What is right is right. She had to know, better to hear it now, and from the horse's mouth. Some day, Apollina, mon belle petite ananas, some day.

CHAPTER 18

Before I was put on the Capability Programme at work; I was arriving early for work, getting through my day without a hitch, staying on a bit later as and when required, and for the most part, exceeding my targets. But now, I'm locked into this negative frequency, a self-perpetuating accelerated mud-slide straight towards Shit Town. When I visited the Citizens Advice Bureau, it looked like they could help me, but whatever they told me, it's been wiped from my brain, like I never went at all, such is the stress. Day by day, the stress is getting worse, I am worrying about it so much that I am hardly sleeping at all – lying in bed, clawing for air; like a concrete slab is on my chest, it just feels heavier and heavier. The snake has nearly swallowed me whole.

It's a catch 22; finally, when I do fall asleep, having been deprived of it all night, I end up falling into a deep, deep sleep, so much so that it has caused me to sleep-in and be late for work, on more than a few occasions recently. I am pretty sure that I am screwed, and my subconscious, rather than pull me up by my boot straps, is kicking me deeper into the dirt. All this worrying pish has got me pickled, at this stage I'd be more use if I just lay down against a door and was paid to be a human draft excluder. It is madness, all of it, when I was doing well at work, Victoria in all her spite, has chosen to screw me over, and now I feel trapped in one giant bubble, filled with anxiety and pish. I feel like a victim, but one day I won't, and in the future when I am on a better footing, I will look back on this time and be sure of one thing, I swear I will never feel this way again.

"I saw that you logged on to your phone at 09:16 this morning Joseph", Victoria says loudly across my team's bank of desks. The fucking arsehole is watching me like a hawk, I cannot afford to keep giving her ammo like this, but if I could only get a good night's sleep. My entire team say nothing, they all just look at each other, they know that I have been selected for the meat grinder, but they don't know why, and there's nothing any of them can do, even if they wanted to. Victoria stays stood there, just mad as a hatter, she isn't even attempting to hide her animosity towards me, "Joseph, meeting room. Right now."

On this occasion, we don't go deep into the heart of the building, where you need senior level clearance just to scratch your arse, this time we go to an office with a clear glass facing that is only a stone throw away from my desk. Victoria wants to put on a show.

There is no fannying about, Victoria is up for war and wades straight in. "Really Joseph? Really?" So aggressive, borderline incoherent, she has really worked herself up for this one. It's only happened to me once or twice before, where I have been faced with someone ferociously angry with me from the off, like I have walked into an argument that I didn't even know that I was part of. It baffled me then, and I am equally as baffled now. Even with the foreknowledge that Victoria is out to get me, I'm still surprised at just how angry she appears.

I just look at Victoria, to talk first would be to justify her lunacy. Even through her fake tan I can see how flushed she is. "I mean, you're not even trying now, are you?" Victoria asks me, so completely full of piss and vinegar. Continuing, "we gave you a chance to save yourself, to prove that you cared about your job here. But you've only gotten worse; turning up late, dressing sloppy, your call-stats dropping off so much it's pathetic. I mean these are facts, it's all here in black and white." I look down, and there on the desk is a single sheet of A4 sized paper, my recent performance "issues" crudely listed in bullet points and written in block capitals.

"Victoria, you have to stop this." I say to her, instinctually sliding the sheet of paper to the side. I am searching, hoping, that in her heart of hearts, Victoria can see sense and put an end to this. "Victoria, this has gone far enough. The only reason that my performance has slipped so much of late is that I have been worrying myself to death. I need this job, and I know that I have done nothing wrong." Victoria, still fizzing, walks over to me, never breaking the gaze of her unblinking velociraptor eyes, and snatches up the piece of paper from the desk. She declares, "Flanagan, me, you, 10am, a week from today."

Victoria walks away towards the door, as she approaches it she glances back at me to have one final pop, a look of complete disgust etched upon her face. "You're so fucking pathetic", before turning the light out as she leaves.

So that's that then, a one-way ticket to Fuckedville. I take stock for a moment, stood there, alone in the darkness, a silhouette against the artificial light of the main office, my nips rock solid under the full blast of the air conditioning. A week from today my fate will be sealed, a week from today I will crash through the floor to an even lower state of existence, and all I will have learned from this – is that some people will choose to crush you, just for the sheer fucking hell of it.

CHAPTER 19

Sat on my bench again, staring at the ground. I actually feel like I could yack, old skool car-sick style. Perhaps I should just let it all swirl and swoosh around in my wee pot-belly and then let it just erupt out of my mouth like a glorious super volcano. Deep breaths, just need to keep breathing. But my eyes keep welling up, I don't think I can hack this anymore, I've been pissing against the wind this whole time; the credit card debt, no pals, and soon to be, no job either.

What am I going to tell my folks? There's every chance that they will throw me out over the debt; darkening their name, destroying their credit rating, and what have I got to show for it? Nothing, absolutely nothing. Pursuing the band, the very thing that I thought would set me free, take me around the world, allow me to meet new and exciting people, is the very thing that has chewed me up.

But has it really? The reality is no, it was the way in which I pursued the band that has left me up shit creek without a paddle, not the dream itself. It's in times like this when I am all anxious, as a coping mechanism I default to day-dreaming; there's a bit of me that wonders if life would be better if it was possible to return to your mother's womb. You could go to her and say, "Mum, a quick word please." She'd look at you, understandably concerned, and say, "hello son, is everything alright?" You would tell her, "look, I've been on this Earth long enough now, and it's abundantly clear that I'm fucking rubbish at it. I don't think that this existence and I are a good fit. So, with your blessing, I'd like to go back."

Your Mum would mull it over, before reluctantly agreeing. "My body isn't what it used to be son" isn't going to cut the mustard. "Mother, you'll be fine – we'll both be just fine", you tell her as you lay the back of your head on her front monkey patch. You close your eyes, and like a guided meditation, you're eased back in without the graphic exposure of your own Mum's fanjanga. You are both at peace; cosy and warm, all shrunken and unobtrusive, basking in the blissful sensation of protection and belonging of your Mammy's womb – ah, magic! But that's a load of old bollocks isn't it, just mind wandering pish.

But it doesn't take much at all for my mind to go wandering, I'll use any old excuse to deny my reality, to procrastinate in doing what needs to be done. It's just all so frustrating; I didn't kill anyone, I didn't wave my nob at kids. I got into a spot of debt and as a result

I am staring down the barrel of losing my twenties to working like a slave in menial jobs, just to get back to what is ordinarily most peoples' starting point. A harsh lesson is being taught here, that is for sure.

I'm not going to yack, but in saying that my eyes are still very watery. Maybe I just need a big cry, a "bollocks to it, let it all out, I don't care how uncomfortable this might make you feel" good old fashioned weep to myself; shuddering shoulders, dreadful snotters everywhere. It is only natural after all, no macho nonsense round this way, I think I will just let it all go, give it the full shebang.

"You alright there, Joe?" Of course, Walter. I hastily wipe my eyes and not so subtly wipe some half-tears-half-snot from my nose and try and clear my throat. "Oh..hi. Hi Walter, how are you doing?" Walter sits down, he takes one look at me and for the first time, in all the times where we have met, he is deadly serious. I can't bring myself to look at him, my face is straining to keep it together as it is. I feel this wave within me, it's no longer nausea, I'm well passed that, it's that strange overwhelming, undeniable, physically induced necessity, to just say your piece, spill your guts, confess your sins.

Here goes. "Walter, I feel ashamed telling you this. I know that you fought in the war and that your life was a million times harder than mine. That is exactly why I have never said anything about this stuff before, but the truth is, you are the only real friend that I have, and I didn't want you to be disappointed in me. Excuse my language, but I fucked it all up, and I've created this black hole for myself that just seems to consume anything vaguely positive that I come into contact with. My pals aren't around anymore because we were in a band together, I thought that we were all on the same page, but we weren't. Then I, like a complete fucking moron, went ahead and racked up as much debt as I could muster on all this equipment. When my pals gave me the news flash that they all had their own plans, I imploded, told them where they could stick their friendship. It has all just snow balled from there; I feel totally isolated, I'm about to get canned at work, I'm crying on a public park bench like the proverbial lost soul. You must think that I am just a big blouse? I wouldn't blame you, I wouldn't blame you at all."

Walter pauses, which is unlike him, as I have only ever associate him with his razor-sharp wit. But perhaps it is because this is the first time that we have not spoken about something so easily disposable – that we are broaching a subject that Walter deems worthy of more in-depth consideration. For the first time I hear

Walter talking fully in a straight tone, with no hint of humour or sarcasm or general carry-on.

"Joe, son. You're right about some things, but very wrong about others. That was a silly thing you did; getting yourself into debt like that. And you're right too about me having a very different life from you when I was your age. But, you're not pathetic. You're in a jam, and inch by inch, you'll get out of it. That's how it goes. Dear Lord, I don't know what the hell is going on with the world these days; all this new technology, so many distractions – I can see why so many people, not just you, are lost. But you just need to keep on at it son. I hate to tell you this, but this world, this life, it owes you nothing. It's up to you to, every day, to just keep putting one foot in front of the other and keep pushing forward. If the war taught me anything, it was that.

In my final days of the war, we knew we were close to victory, but nothing had been certain up until that point, so no one was taking anything for granted. I was part of a parachute regiment to be dropped into occupied France to take on the Nazis at close quarters.

I will never forget for as long as I live, the sights and the sounds as I leapt from that plane. It was as though I was drifting through purgatory, heading straight down into the bowels of hell. Amidst the unholy mass before me, my heart pounding out of my chest, it seemed impossible that I would survive, such was the sheer ferocity before me. Floating down to Earth in my parachute, I thought of how unnatural it was to be up there; having jumped out of a plane, to land in some foreign country, to kill my fellow man, or be killed. How unnatural, all of it, the whole bloody unnatural mess.

As each second passed, avoiding being killed, it felt like I was defying the odds. I landed in some woods, somehow managing to avoid sustaining any kind of injury on the way down. The woods provided me some much sought-after cover, but I was alone. There in the darkness, I had to press onwards, but I was unsure in which direction to go. All around me was the sound of machine gun fire and explosions, in that moment, all I knew for certain was that I would not be alone for long.

Then, for the briefest of moments, there was silence, and in that short window of time, as crazy as it sounds, a sense of calm came over me. It was so peculiar; such a contrasting state of mind from everything I had been feeling up until that point.

And just then, I heard the cracking of a branch – a German soldier and I had been stood right next to each other, completely unaware of the other's presence, until now. He had noticed me only a split-second before I had noticed him. Charging at my waist, he cleared me out, knocking me to the ground.

We rolled and tussled and barked and snarled – every muscle, every fibre of my being, engaged, locked in the most primitive way a person can be – when fighting for their life. He reached down and grabbed a dagger from his boot, in doing so, it provided me with the opportunity to free my arm and grab his wrist, holding him off, but I was not sure for how long. I managed to angle my knee up to his chest and gain enough leverage to kick him off me. I reached for my side arm to shoot the bastard, but before I had the chance we were both blown completely off of our feet. Artillery fire – how I wasn't blown to bits or battered to death against a tree, I don't know.

My entire body aching, dazed, I frantically searched the ground, desperately trying to find my revolver, but I couldn't see it anywhere. Then it dawned on me, to look around for my foe. If I had survived that artillery blast, then he could have also.

Surrounding explosions shed intermittent light upon me. I continued to scan the terrain for him, looking for any kind of weapon. To my absolute euphoria, I noticed a German MP 40 machine gun lying on the ground. I ran to it and scooped it up, only to feel a pain that I had never felt before or since. The handle was red hot, and I had grasped it with all my might. Instinctually, I squeezed my right wrist with my left hand, attempting to alleviate the pain, but regardless, I had to carry on, I had to keep my eyes open and my head up.

Then there he was, only about twenty feet away. Breathing heavily, and like me, just a boy, bloodied and blackened. The knife in his hand, stood there sizing me up, knowing what he had to do, his eyes welled up with tears.

By now, such was the increasing frequency and proximity of the surrounding battle, although it was at night, it was as though we were cast in daylight. I stare at his hand, I see it grip tighter on the handle of his dagger, his face contorted with pure animalistic rage. He let out one final almighty battle cry, and then charged.

That was the last I saw of him. Before he got to me, another artillery blast went off, this one even closer than the last. I was breathing, I knew that much. My body was aching; like I had been kicked and punched on every single part of my body. I began to doze in, then back out, of consciousness. The pain then began to fade, I was sure that I was dying, I just wanted to go to sleep, to dream of my Rose, Mother too – I was sure that soon I would be reunited with father. Still, lying in the mud, I accepted my fate, I closed my eyes.

"You OK buddy?" A voice, in what I presume is an American accent. A hand then reaches out and gives me a shake, then asked once more, "buddy, you OK?" I can only muster a mumble in reply. "Can you open your eyes?" He asks me. I manage to look up, and there standing over me is a figure, a silhouette against the light of the battle-filled sky. I cannot see his face, his features hidden to me. I presume that as I could at least open my eyes, he must have thought I had a chance of surviving. He must have been a strapping lad, as he reached down, picked me up, and carried me over his shoulder, reassuringly informing me, "we're getting you out of here." Hunched over, my arms lifelessly free and swaying as he carried me, the desire to sleep was almost too much, the blood rushing to my head, it was the most vulnerable I have ever been.

I don't know how long he was carrying me for, but I only came back around fully as I was being placed down on the ground next to a medic. As he turned to go, I whispered, "thank you. What's your name?" As he ran back towards the woods, he shouted over his shoulder, "you're welcome. The name's Mulligan." And before I knew it, he had vanished into the woods.

I never found out what happened to him, or what regiment he belonged to. There were a lot of US and Canadian troops involved that day, so I'm not even sure where he came from. But that man is the reason I'm sitting here with you today, and there is not a day that goes by where I do not think about him, and how much I owe him. Although, despite all the odds, when I was recovering in hospital, someone, somehow, managed to find my revolver, that was 'sweetheart gripped' with a photo of my Rose, and return it to me. It was like a miracle, a sign from God.

I know that was then, and this is now, and everything is different these days. I'm not saying that you have to experience war or anything like that, but the principles of what happened to me are the same. When you are in a hell of a situation; you just have to keep working, keep fighting, keep pushing, and eventually your break will come, good people will seek you out and help you, you'll learn along the way, and in time you will be able to look back and know, that when the all hope seemed lost, you came through, and now you can handle anything."

Fuck me, what a story – it shifts me like I have just taken a .42 carat diamond perspective bullet to the brain. I mean, what a gift; for Walter to open up like that, and share that with me. I feel a true sense of gratitude in being able to hear that. "Thanks Walter. You know what? I'm going to go into that meeting at work with my head held high, no matter the outcome, and just take it from there." Walter, pleased to see a bit of fire in my belly, "Joe, you tell the bastards."

Walter has really got me there. He's right; this isn't it, there is no death sentence, the world doesn't stop turning. I will make it through – sooner or later, one way or another.

CHAPTER 20

I arrive at work early, around 07:30, which is by far the earliest I have ever been near the place. I couldn't stomach a breakfast before I left the house as the result of having taken a horrific nervous death-shit as soon as I woke up, thus spooking me and squashing my appetite. I opted for a strong cup of tea with two sugars, this way, no matter what happens I won't have the indignity of turning into a rubber man because of my blood sugar crashing.

By now, people in my team, and the few others in here that knows me, will be fully aware that today I have my big meeting, judgement day. I can't be seen in my usual office, instead I opt to hide out on the top floor, where I have never been before, until I have to come back down for the meeting at 10:00.

The top floor is a strange isolated place, filled with random office clutter. There I can pace up and down one single stretch of corridor, going over and over again in my mind if there is anything that I can do, anything at all to stop the axe from falling on me. Ever since Victoria set this shit-show in motion, the crushing sense of injustice and stress of wondering what I'll do next has been like a slow trudge into a quicksand of negativity in my mind; a self-fulfilling prophecy that I am going to go into this meeting and have to listen to them go through their spiel, as carefree, Flanagan and Victoria toy with my livelihood like a cat playing with a dead small bird, before they deliver their verdict, get my arse out of here, and conclude this sorry episode.

I go to the Gents' toilets, I wash my face under the cold tap, I straighten my tie, and for a moment I pause to just take in the face looking back at me; tired, jaded, afraid. I grab a bundle of paper towels from the dispenser and I quickly dry my face, got to go, there's no point in delaying the inevitable. I just keep reminding myself of the advice that Walter gave me; to just face this, as I will survive it, and regardless of my fear and anxiety, I will go on. No matter what, I will make it through, and just go again.

Time drags by, but eventually I have to make my move. I get in the lift, making my way back down to my office. As I walk through the office floor towards the meeting rooms at the back, I can see my team all looking at me. I do not avert my gaze, I just keep moving forward, chin up all the way. There, desperate to swipe me through the security doors, is Victoria. That fucking face of hers, yet again, she is struggling to contain her smug self-satisfaction.

I am shown to an office I have never been to before, it could be a complete coincidence, but this meeting room is positioned alarmingly close to an exit door that I didn't even know existed, that I can see through the window, leads straight out onto a side street. I guess this is where they take you when they want you to get to leave ASAP without making a scene in front of the main offices; just in case you cry, or stick the nut in them or fucking wreck the place.

I walk into the meeting room and I am immediately greeted by Flanagan, he stands up for just a moment as he tells me, "Joseph, please take a seat." Flanagan sits back down again, Victoria takes a seat next to him and despite the formality of the situation, she is still beaming; radiating pure shittyness. Sat in the corner of the room is a strange looking middle-aged woman with a kind of 1970s bowl-cut fringe, with librarian-esque specs sat on the tip of her nose. Flanagan informs me, "this is Trish, Trish will be recording the minutes of our discussion for our records." Flanagan takes a moment to scan over his paperwork, I can't help but think, "get a move on, lets get this pish over and done with. And, by the way, how can it only be about 10:05 and the shoulders of your suit are already coated in dandruff?"

Flanagan runs his finger over the last line of the paperwork in front of him before discouragingly making an "mmmh" noise. Followed up by, "not ideal Joseph, eh? This here; these notes; poor time keeping, your targets slipping. When we spoke before, I clearly explained this process to you, and the potential ramifications of a poor performance during this assessment period, did I not?" My throat, as dry as a desert sandal, limits me to the most basic muttering of "yes." Flanagan appears to be just about to continue with his usual formal scripted mad mince, when he self corrects. "Joseph, look, this won't take long. I have gone over your performance reports for the past few weeks and it paints a pretty clear picture. But before you take a short break, while Victoria and I deliberate on matters, are there any reasons that you would like to state for the record, why you have performed so poorly, these last few weeks in particular?" The fucking gall of this prick. I clear my throat as I loosen my tie, my voice lower and quieter than normal, I reply. "It's just been all of this, you know? The stress, you know, it's..." And at that, Flanagan cuts me off. "Alright Joseph, I understand. Now, if you would please excuse us. It's coming up for 10:10, come back, say, at 10:30." I get up from my chair and make my way to the door, I glance back for just a moment as I open the door, Flanagan has got his head back into my notes and Victoria, Victoria is fucking smiling at me.

I close the door of the meeting room and head down the corridor, a dead man walking. There is nowhere for me to go, I don't have a security pass to get me through the doors to go anywhere. I will have to spend the next ten minutes wandering about in this limited space like some tortured manically depressed ghoul. I look over to the door that leads on to the street, knowing, knowing that any time soon I'll be forced to make the wank walk; the just been canned walk, the out on my arse walk.

"Hello Joe." I hear from a female voice coming from behind me. I turn around to see that it is Joyce. Lovely Joyce, my golden lady, am I glad to see her. Without hesitation, I give her a big hug, holding on in there probably a few seconds longer than would ever be appropriate. "Are you okay, Joe?" Joyce asks me, curious as to why I embraced her so intensely. For a moment, I contemplate unloading all my psychic dung on her, but I opt against it, it's the first time that I have seen Joyce in ages, instead, I want to find out how she's doing. "Joyce, it's great to see you. How are you keeping?" Joyce smiles back at me. "Oh, it's not been easy Joe. I have had a terrible time with my Crohn's, but I am on different medication now and I am feeling a lot better." That is good, Joyce is a good'un. "What are you doing through here anyways?" Joyce asks me inquisitively. Again, why burden her with my woe-bomb, "oh, eh, just a meeting thing that I have been asked to attend. I thought that I would pop out for a bit and stretch my legs." Joyce looks at me as if to say, "don't bullshit a bullshitter." Quickly changing tact, Joyce says to me. "Actually, I am glad that I bumped into you. I have your ped." That is nice and all, but that's like saying you found the Captain of the Titanic's favourite pair of slippers; a brief comfort, before a cold harsh sinking. Still not wanting to bum Joyce out, I feign excitement at this development, as it is completely inconsequential now. I comment, "a day late and a dollar short." Joyce seeking to clarify what I said, "sorry Joe, what was that?" I think I may have come across like a bit of a dickhead there. Joyce is a legend, I can't be upsetting her. Sheepishly I reply, "nothing Joyce, just ignore me, I'm just mumbling nonsense to myself."

Then it hits me. Oh – my – fucking word. The ped, the fucking ped. I threw everything in there. I need to see it. "Joyce. Please, help me." Joyce looks at me as though I have been struck by lightening right before her very eyes. "Of course, Joe, anything. What can I do?" Joyce asks, clearly ready and willing to support me in this, what must look like a peculiar moment. It is time to fill Joyce in.

"Here's what's going down – that mad bitch Victoria has set me up and I am just about to be tossed out of here on my arse. There is a chance, no matter how small, that contained within my ped are the copies of my monthly reviews that will get me out of all of this, by proving that Victoria doctored them to get me fired. All because I refused her advances, if you can believe that crazy shit. But we need to move now." Joyce, moves her eyeballs from side to side, quickly processing everything that I have just told her, before nodding her head and standing up straight. "I knew she had a thing for you. Let's go Joe, I never liked that cunt anyways." That a girl Joyce! "Joyce, you're a legend."

Joyce scans us through into the main office and we make a beeline to her desk. We arrive at Joyce's work station and there it is, my ped; tucked in under her desk. Joyce stands guard as I frantically slide the main drawer of my ped open, I dig through all the mess and nonsense, desperately looking for the pale blue trace copies of my monthly reports. And there they are, it is better than I could have imagined; TEN MONTHS' WORTH. Shaking, "Joyce, this is it. This is really it." Joyce is delighted for me, but she brings me back around soon enough. "Joe, OK, so what do we do now?" She's right. I can't just walk back into the meeting, waving these documents around; Flanagan could just grab them off me and set them on fire, Victoria could eat them or shove them up her chuff, who knows what might happen, anything could happen.

Think Joe, think! Ah ha, I have got it. "Joyce, to the copier!" Joyce and I make our way to the copy room. "What is the plan Joe?" Joyce asks, well and truly swept up in my shot at redemption. Laser focused, I explain exactly what we are going to do. "Joyce, we are running out of time. First, I am going to make a colour photocopy of all ten of these, and I am going to take them back into the meeting with me. While I am doing that, I need you to scan all the documents and email them to me, use your personal email account; I don't want some forensic I.T gimp going through your work email account and getting you into trouble. But most importantly, once you have scanned and emailed them to me, I need you to take the original documents and stash them somewhere; your car, anywhere. We good?" Joyce, firmly plants her hand on my shoulder and declares, "I've got you Joe."

I gather my photocopies, Joyce hands me her security pass. "Go Joe, leave this to me. Quickly, go." I get to the rear of the office and scan my way back into the meeting room area, using Joyce's security pass. I make it through in the absolute nick of time, just as

Victoria has reopened the door to let me in. I slip Joyce's security pass into my back pocket, making sure that no one sees it, as if anyone ever found out that she had let me use it, especially while helping me in trying to take down *The Man*, then Joyce would be in a whole heap of trouble too.

I see Victoria looking at the pieces of paper in my hand with mild suspicion, clearly confused as to where I could have acquired them, given that I was only permitted to wander a small area during the short break, given my limited security clearance.

Regardless, once more, Flanagan dryly ushers me in and asks me to take a seat, as Trish sits primed, ready to recommence her note taking. Flanagan recommences our meeting, "Joseph, Victoria and I have had the opportunity to have one final recap of all the key issues regarding your employment with the company, and it is with great regret that I have to inform you..." "Shut up." Just like that, it just popped out of me. Completely flabbergasted, Flanagan leans forward to listen closer, as if his ears had deceived him the first time around. "Excuse me?", Flanagan enquires, completely astonished. Then there it was, that fire inside me, that fire that had been like a distant whimper in a deep dark cave within my soul, was back, and it was now old testament super napalm, and these two mother fuckers were about to get it.

"I said, Flanagan, shut up. For once in your boring crusty fucking life, shut your fucking mouth." Incensed, Flanagan pops up and yells at me, "get out! Right now! You're fired!" I let out a nervous giggle, I look over to Victoria, she's completely bewildered as to what is going on.

"Flanagan, pussy cat. Sit down." Flanagan is just about to erupt in reply, when I calmly add, "trust me, it's in yours, and your bosses' interests that you hear what I have to say, to give you the opportunity to rectify this, before things get really out of hand." Reluctantly, Flanagan sits down, and Victoria begins to squirm more and more in her chair.

"You see, what I have here are copies of my monthly reviews – the original authentic reviews, before Victoria submitted doctored versions, that ultimately led to, you know, all of this carry on." I slide them over to Flanagan. "Look at them for yourself. They clearly show that not only was I not under-performing, I was in-fact performing well above average." Victoria pipes in, "rubbish Joe, you're talking rubbish." But I don't even get a chance to reply to

Victoria, as Flanagan gets there first to firmly tell her, "be quiet, Victoria!"

Flanagan quickly scans through a few of the photocopies, clearly growing more and more concerned with every word. "This, this is very serious. Victoria, why on Earth would you do this?" Victoria, like a rabbit caught in the headlights. "Come on, who are you going to believe?" For the first time, I see colour in Flanagan's face, and it is bright red. Enraged, Flanagan continues to flick through the documents, faster and faster, "it's all here Victoria, how could you have been so stupid? Head Office have spent a fortune on you and look what you have done. And for fucks sake Trish, stop typing!" Trish freezes, now very much aware that she is witness to a good old fashioned bit of scandal.

Victoria looks as though she is about to cry, Trish looks as though she wants to pull a parachute chord and get the hell of there, and as for Flanagan, he places his hands firmly on his bowed head as he stairs down in disbelief at the complete orgy of incriminating paperwork. There is no way I can stay in this job now, but I'm leaving on my terms. Flanagan slowly looks up at me, dazed, eyes the size of saucers; like a rabbit in the headlights. It is time to cease my opportunity. "Flanagan. Let's get straight to the point here. Your golden girl has royally fucked up, her coo-bag pals in HR were very likely in on it, and if you don't get your cheque book out right now, I'll go to the press. I can see it now – 'insurance wankers spunk fortune on poster girl who, as it so happens, is a nasty manipulative horrible bastard.' Not as punchy as your usual tabloid muck, but you get the point." Flanagan, visibly wounded by my demands, pleads to me, "come on Joseph, you know I don't have that kind of authority." To see them cooking where they sit; like eggs on a fryer, it's glorious. This is no time to fuck about, I tell Flanagan, "you have ten minutes. I'll wait right here." Flanagan frantically scoops up all the paperwork, and ushers his colleagues to follow him, "come on, we're going. Move your arse!" Alone in the room, my head is spinning. What a rush, there I was, down and out less than half an hour ago, and now it feels like anything could happen – that finally, I won't be eaten up by all of this.

Ten minutes pass by, I think to myself, "that's that then. Fuck them." And just as I am about to open the door to leave, Flanagan comes bungling in. Completely out of breath, he must have been running around like a total mad arsehole. Pausing between words as he tries desperately to compose himself, I notice that Flanagan has something in his hand, an envelope. "Joe. I. I have. I have had a word with someone at the very. The very highest level. At Head Quarters. In my hand, is a written offer – you leave here today having signed this document, stating that you won't go to the press or speak of this to anyone – and in return we will make a payment to you of five times your annual salary." Fuck. Me. Flanagan offers me the piece of paper – I snatch it out of his hand and begin to speed-read. There it is, an offer too good to refuse – I can pay off my debt, I get out of here – this document is a shot at a fresh start.

Completely aghast by the whole situation and clearly looking like a defeated man, Flanagan quietly pleads, "I guarantee you – sign this now, and the money will be in your account by close of play today." No messing; I slap the letter down on the desk, I sign it in a micro second, before giving it straight back to him. Flanagan, while still visibly shaken, looks relieved slightly; my signing the document being the first step in putting this episode to bed.

Flanagan folds the letter and places it in his inside suit pocket. "Now, if you would please Joe…" Flanagan says, as he opens his body to direct me to the side door, AKA the "don't make a scene door." What a dick, no way. "Flanagan, I'm not leaving through your sneaky side door. Scan me into the main office."

Reluctantly, Flanagan scans me through into the main office, before immediately retreating to the inner bowels of the building, surely to conduct a further post-mortem of the morning's events. Joyce comes straight towards me, she demands to know. "What happened Joe?" Beaming, I tell her, "we won Joyce, we won." I grab her by the waist, lean her back and give her a massive kiss on the lips. When I pull away, Joyce looks stunned. I remove Joyce's security pass from my pocket and place it in her hand. "Joyce, that's me, I'm going now, I'm free. For reasons that will become clear, I can't tell you everything that I want to tell you right now – we'll meet soon, I'll get the original documents from you, and I will give you the full low-down. Thanks for everything, I don't know how I could ever repay you." I could give her some of my new lovely money, but then again, steady on. Joyce, blushing, gives me a big hug and tells me, "it was my pleasure Joe, now go get em'."

I strut through the offices. For the first time, it appears that people seem to be noticing me. I burst through main entrance doors and make my way outside to the walkway that leads onto the main street. I pause for a moment, I take out my phone and text Apollina: "Hi. I am sorry about the other day.

Great news, I have sorted everything.

Can I make it up to you? I would like to take you to dinner, anywhere you want, it's on me. I will explain fully if/when we meet up. Joe x."

The sun is shining, what a day. I feel so alive

Just then, I hear someone loudly yell, "Van Keefe", followed by the screeching of tyres.

BANG!

I'm laid out, the back of my head aches. I feel fresh air kissing the innards of my chest, it's like I'm winded, but much worse.

Oh my God. I think I've been shot.

What the fuck?

I've been shot.

I think I'm dying.

CHAPTER 21

Eyes locked shut. A complete state of peace. I have no spatial awareness – am I still matter, or am I now a boundless stream of particles, travelling through infinity, in some new abstract incarnation, in some unknown dimension? I could not tell you if I am nestled safely on the bed of an ocean on some distant world, or if I am high above the clouds, just gliding without obstruction, wrapped in a sense of unbending certainty that no harm will come to me here, wherever here is.

Yet, I still cannot see anything, all I know for certain is that I am at peace. Every now and then I hear voices, my Mum and Dad, my brother, Andrew, and at one stage I thought I even heard Walter, but their voices are distant, muffled and infrequent. If I am dead, is this it? How long have I been in this place? My concept of time has become meaningless, intangible, silly almost.

However long it has been, I feel as though I have been separated from my body; like I am just a brain in a glass jar. If this is the case, I want a tremendous cyborg body to go with it; rocket launchers, flame throwers, the full shooting match. However, more and more I feel like I am able to grasp onto my thoughts for longer, and coincidentally, hints of my physical being are returning also. I have felt hunger, like I need to go pee, like I could do one of my big nervous farts, and a general overall feeling of weakness. The weakness, the fatigue, it swirls in me, I feel delirious for brief spells, then I seem to check out for a bit.

I am beginning to hear the sound of voices more and more frequently; the murmuring of strangers' talking, and again; my Mum and Dad, Andrew, and Walter. I can certainly hear Walter, he is the loudest yet, I can hear him, it's so loud, "son!"

Eyes open. Ugh, fuck-ing hell. Ugh, I think I am going to spew, I feel dreadful. I am in bed, I have no idea where though, I go to lean over the bed, should I actually throw up, but it's far too sore. Aaargh! You mother fucker! I am in absolutely agony. I am consumed by an extreme pain all over my torso; far worse than being winded. Where has my state of blissful floaty nothingness gone? You absolute coo-bag, I need help, I need drugs, I need smacked over the head with a fucking didgeridoo or a giant frying pan, something, anything.

"He's awake!" A voice decrees from across the room. It's a nurse, hello cheeky. "Doctor Bünter, come quick." Within moments a doctor is at my bedside, checking my pulse, then my forehead. "Good morning Joe. Good to see you, bright and alert. You are in the Royal Alexandria Hospital. How are you feeling?" Making an o-face, trying not to bean-up everywhere, "I'm sore doc, really sore." Dr Bünter nods empathetically, "don't worry Joe, our nurses will sort you out with something for the pain just now. Joe, you my friend have been shot."

What? How can this be? Shot? Who has a gun in Scotland, except farmers and about eight proper bad guys? Shot, shot? This is fucking nuts, who would shoot me? Well, apart from Flanagan and Victoria. But I thought the majority of scumbags were knife carrying horrible bastards. Dr Bünter continues, "the bullet entered the right side of your chest, ricocheted off your right shoulder blade and exited your body, just under your right arm pit. All things considered, you are a very lucky boy." Lucky, is this guy for real, lucky? For someone involved in zero gang or drug related shenanigans, in a country where almost no one has a gun, to get shot, I'd say is really, *really* unlucky. I peer down, I look like I am made of papier mache; completely wrapped in a cast from the waist up. The nurse comes over with the pain killers, taking the cap off the tube inserted in my hand, she fires it straight in there. The drugs enter my blood stream like a freight train, jeezo, that's quick, these drugs are magic. Whee! Magic shoes, cats, football faces, laser lights disco iglu rave bunker, pumpkin tits. Zzzzz.

Pfft, that was a good sleep, a solid ten. It must be the drugs they gave me, perhaps I slept almost too well; my head feels full of cotton wool; pure mung. I put my hand on the bedside table to get a better sense of my bearings, there I find my contact lenses case. Opening it up, I quickly pop my them in, my eyes feeling tender, probably because I have been lens-free for however long I have been in here. "Hello Joseph", says a very formal voice from the corner of the room. I'm struggling to focus properly, as stellar as those drugs were, I am a bit fucked up here, in kind of a nice way. Two figures approach me, in a brief moment of heightened paranoia I wonder if it is the guys who shot me, here to finish me off, but such are the drugs, I don't care, I'm totally cabbaged. "I'm Detective Sergeant MacDermid, and this is my colleague, Detective Constable, MacArthur." I can't help but think "the two Macs", like they are the stars of some masonic buddy cop movie. The Detective Sergeant continues, "you are a lucky boy Joseph, or unlucky, depending how you look at it." Unlucky, definitely unlucky. "You see, you have survived a short-range gunshot to the chest." Bit by bit the fogginess is lifting, I reply, "yeah, the doc was telling me that..." And before I have the chance to continue Detective Constable, MacArthur, interrupts me. "What is your relationship to Marco Van Keefe?" Van Keefe, why are they asking me about that tadger? I have absolutely nothing to hide here. "Van Keefe, sure, I know who he is. He's just some guy from my work. I think I've spoken to him once, twice tops — he's a cocky guy, the general consensus is that the birds are bonkers for him, a top shagger by all accounts." Detective Constable, MacArthur nods in acknowledgement, before explaining to me, "It's funny that you should mention his reputation in relation to women, Joe — Van Keefe is currently in protective custody. Joe, to clarify, you have been the victim of mistaken identity." Mistaken identity? As bizarre as it seems, I'm actually kind of flattered. Detective Sergeant MacDermid takes over, "it would appear that Mr Van Keefe has been befriending the pretty wife of a senior gangland figure. The gentleman in question found out, and as an act of retribution he set about eliminating Mr Van Keefe, and shot you by mistake." Jeezo, I don't believe this — not only am I getting no action, I have been shot, shot with an actual gun, on the account of someone else's shagging action. It's unbelievable.

Like the solid buddy cop duo that I consider these guys to be, the questioning is once more passed back to Detective

Constable, MacArthur. "What do you remember about the day of the incident?" There is no point telling them about my work dramas, that has nothing to do with this. "I was leaving work, I didn't see anyone, all I heard was a car moving off quickly and someone shout 'Van Keefe.' The next thing I know I am on my back, and then I woke up here. That's all I know." For a split second, yet another mad moment of paranoia creeps in; that somehow I might be able to give them more info, despite having no more to offer, probably brought on by an underlying nervousness of being completely debilitated in the presence of two senior coppers, something I have never experienced before.

Both detectives look at each other in quiet resignation, certain that I have told them all I know – they know what happened and why, and that I have no nothing on the mad daft bastard perpetrators who did this to me. Detective Constable, MacArthur concludes matters by informing me, "thank you for your time Joe, and get well soon. We have your contact details should we need to ask you any further questions, and we will keep you informed of any developments, as and when we can." I want absolute jack-nanty to do with this. A court case? With armed gangland figures? Get that to absolute fuck. I saw nothing, and I will say nothing.

Both detectives leave, and as they make their way down the corridor, I hear one of them say, "he's awake, if you want to go in and see him." I hear steps quicken before my Mum and Dad burst through the ward doors. "Joe!" screams my Mum, before sobbing like a maniac. Mum proceeds to make a series of high-pitched noises amidst an eruption of tears and snotters as she peppers my head with kisses. Even my Dad has a tear in his eye, as irrationally, he pats random parts of me, in case there are any wounds on me that have gone unnoticed by the medical staff.

Not much is said really, it's just a big teary group hug, as not only is this the first time that my folks have seen me since I came around, I am getting a sense of what has happened, the magnitude of it all, and the trauma is creeping in a bit. We could have been closer as a family these past few years, but I am still their boy, and I am glad that they did not have to go through having to bury me. As much as I feel that I have sleep walked into my current family dynamic, I think we all have in some respects; especially when it comes to trying to connect with each other, taking an interest in each other and what we are up to, and showing signs of affection, when all is said and done, we're still family.

We compose ourselves eventually, the box of paper hankies by the bed has taken a battering. Mum asks if her make-up is okay as she dabs her eyes, before adding, "Your big brother flew home to see you. He was here two days ago, but he had to go, a big conference to go to. You know how it is. He has asked me to text him with any updates." Haha, superb, Andrew, the golden balled golden boy, I reckon that I would have to be frantically analized by an extra-terrestrial, live on TV, and then set on fire and propelled out of a circus cannon, for him to put his career on hold and make more than his annual cameo appearance. But hey, the fact that he came to see me at all is something, I guess.

Finally, Dad pipes in, "oh, and another thing", pleased that he has remembered something I should know about. "We have had people from the press bombarding us at the house, looking for a statement and such. We told them to bugger off. However, there have been two men from your work who have been most persistent. They are very keen to speak to you straight away. They are here, they are outside in the corridor. Do you want to speak to them?" This is all a bit much, I am not so sure that I want to do this – dealing with coppers and then the emotional slushfest with my parents. But then again, this has all been one big mad surreal episode, perhaps if I speak to these goons and just get it out of the way, then I will be free to get some rest and hopefully some more of those lovely drugs. "Aye, OK Dad, tell them to come in."

Mum gives me one last big hug and my Dad pats me on the head before they make their way out. Once again, I hear steps walking down the corridor towards me. However, whoever is outside stops just before the door, I can hear whispering, whoever is there, some conferring is going down.

The door opens and it's Flanagan from work, accompanied by a well-dressed middle-aged man – tanned hands, an expensive looking wedding ring, designer shoes by the looks of it. My initial impression is that this is not your average grey-aura corporate gimp, this guy looks like a senior tiger-type character.

The sharp suited cat opens proceedings, "Hiya Joe. How are you pal?" Said with all the sincerity of a child entertainer sex pest. I don't want to be openly hostile immediately, but there is a burning desire to be savagely sarcastic to this bell-end. I have been shot in the chest as the result of someone else's nantang action, how the fuck does he think I feel? "Eh, I'm a bit sore", I say meekly in the interest of politeness. Flanagan, as cold as the carcass of a splattered fox on the M8 motorway, "hello Joseph." I bet he is fucking raging that I survived, prick that he is.

The mystery pimp pulls up a chair and sits a bit too close to me. In reply to this aggressive act of body language chess, I retort by slowly reaching for the emergency button hand-piece. I do so with my right arm, it hurts like an absolute bitch to do so, but I grit my teeth to get it none the less.

Captain Flash here, glances at my thumb hovering over the emergency button. He gets it, he knows that I sense he is not so much a tiger, but a wolf in sheep's clothing. He refocuses, gets back into character. "Don't let the accent fool you Joe", he says to me in a broad Yorkshire accent, before continuing, "I'm from head quarters in London. I'm Ted Crumpet." Hold on. What? HQ have sent down their big (passive aggressive) gun, and his name is Crumpet, Ted fucking Crumpet. Regardless of what he has to say, this guy better start talking in some magical mind-bending language, understandable to all, like Jesus, if I am to overcome *that* name. He takes a breath as he attempts to continue speaking, when I interrupt him. "I'm sorry. Crumpet, your name is Ted *Crumpet*?" Crumpet smiles a serial killer grin, trying his damnedest to mask his disdain for me and my mocking of his name. Staying in character, he attempts to brush me off. "It is quite okay Joe, I get it all the time, it's 'Crumpitt', C – R – U – M – P – I – with a a double T at the end." Oh, I see, the double T makes it alright then. This guy is a massive T – I – T – T.

Flanagan, sat in the corner, has said nothing since saying "hello", he's just slumped in the corner like some pathetic cuckhold; his nob in one of those bizarre padlocked cock-locks that denies hard-ons, that Crumpet probably has the key for.

Our Ted here, looks over his shoulder, making sure that none of the doctors or nurses are within ear-shot – playtime regarding his stupid fucking name is over, the shitty fake smile drops from his face, he has come all the way here from London on a mission.

"Look Joe, I won't take up any more of your time than I have to, so I will be brief. Mr Flanagan here has informed my bosses and I of everything that went on with that lass, and how you had positioned yourself with regards to compensation." I like how he described that there, credit where it is due. Captain Crumpet continues, "and I know that you were able to negotiate a sizeable sum in compensation." Then there it is, his mask of decency slips, the first signs of a chink in his armour; as he begins to grit his teeth, the deeper he goes into matters. "So, you walk out the door, which is all well and good, but then you go and get shot on company property. Somehow you inexplicably manage to get yourself involved in two monumental, if you'll excuse my French, cluster fucks, within the space of fifteen minutes. I mean, had you walked another 12 feet you would have been off our premises and on the street, and we would all be in a completely different position to the scenario we currently find ourselves in." What a cock, the next time I get shot I'll be sure to do so in a location that causes no corporate liability. "Being that as it may, if the press were ever to catch wind of our poster girl being a manipulative so-and-so, on top of you then being gunned down because another of our employees was shagging some gangland tart, it's potentially catastrophic for the company's image. I am here on behalf of the Senior Directors to make this all go away. I have in my pocket a written offer, that in exchange for your complete silence on all matters relating to the company; Victoria, the shooting, any of it – we will make you a one-off payment of four hundred thousand pounds."

I nearly choke on my own saliva. FOUR HUNDRED THOUSAND POUNDS. This makes the deal that Flanagan offered me look like the steam off his pish. Crumpet takes an envelope out of the inside pocket of his coat and hands it to me. It's two pages and seven paragraphs of legal wank speak — basically, it reads, "shut the fuck up, take the money, and never darken our door again."

I cannot fully articulate the depths of depravity that I would endure for that sum of money. I summon Flanagan over and ask him to turn around and squat down so that I can use his back as somewhere to write my signature. Crumpet hands me an expensive looking pen, the angle that Flanagan is positioned, it is too sore for me to turn slightly and use my right hand, so with all the grace and accuracy of a drunken cat, I scribble my name using my left hand.

Oor' Ted takes the document from me, then once more reaches into his inside suit pocket and hands me a large crisp cheque. "Joe, I won't keep you. Let's never do this again." Crumpet makes his way to the door, Flanagan still kneeling down, Crumpet turns to him and disdainfully instructs him to "get up." Flanagan gets to his feet and then shuffles out of the door.

I lay back on the bed, clutching the cheque tighter than anything I have ever held. I rub my face up and down with my left hand, I don't know how to act, it's all so overwhelming. I am free. For a while there I was certain that I would fall down the cracks, just another victim of the capitalist meat grinder, but now I have a shot at redemption – the opportunity to move on, a fresh start. I won't fuck it up this time; now I can go to college then university, or go travelling, or start a business if I wanted to. I can do whatever I want, with no financial baggage for me or my family, the only baggage that I will carry, is what I allow myself to carry around my head.

CHAPTER 22

The smell of paint, although sometimes nauseating, it has the capacity to inspire feelings of newness; with each application, evidence of wear and tear is removed, and brightness and freshness reigns supreme. It only took one large tin of white paint to give my entire bedroom two coats. I am chuffed with the job I've done; I really took my time to cover all the skirting boards and the light switch, and make sure that no matter what, I didn't get any on the carpet.

My guitars, they've been polished, put in their cases and flung up the loft. Once more, I am stood in my room stuffing bin bags, but this time I am not filling them with my boatload of pornography, but my clothes. My dreadful clothes, just like me, are moving on and getting a new start too; off to the charity shop they'll go – everything else has been binned. I wanted to leave the place spick and span so that my folks can do what they want with it. My old shite car, I got it picked up by the local scrappy. It only cost me fifty quid to get it to absolute fuck, off to be crushed and recycled into God knows what, something useful I hope.

I am still kind of stunned – it has been a crazy few weeks. I am unsure how to process things, but in a nice way, as although I was shot, I barely remember anything to do with it; my recovery is the only thing fresh in my mind. I keep checking my bank balance via telephone banking, and there it is; the best part of four hundred thousand lovely pounds. I phoned a tax guru, and he said that because of the nature of the payment, it is tax exempt – it's all for me, to use as I please. When listening to the robot woman on the telephone banking read out my balance, I must have hit the repeat option about twenty times, just to hear it again and again, to keep making sure that it's real. I'll probably be doing this for months.

I was teetering on the brink, now I am crying tears of joy, but more so of relief; as one by one I have phoned up my credit card companies, paid them off, and then cut the bastarding cards up, bar one. "One only credit card at a time" will be the rule from now on.

I will put a fair old chunk of change in Mum and Dad's account, although Andrew can sing for it. I'll give Walter's crowd some money towards their trips, and I'll need to get my thinking cap on for what I am going to buy Joyce.

Which reminds me, Joyce text me to say that in amongst the rest of the paper work in my ped, was a photocopy of both sides of Victoria's company credit card. I had totally forgotten that she had asked me to organise a couple of hotel stays for her a while back, and that I should make a copy of her payment details for any future trips. I don't want to risk my legal agreement with the company and jeopardise my dosh, but the devilment in me is tempted to go to an internet café somewhere that isn't local, wear a disguise, log on to some freaky sex website, order some absolutely mental gear, and have it sent to her at work. Just imagining her having to explain to the Finance Department and HR, how she ordered an XXXL butt-plug, nipple clamps, and a three-pack of edible panties, on the company's coin, and then to have it delivered to the office, is a glorious prospect. But nah, time to move on. In years to come, the memory of Victoria, and her mad face, will be a mere distant echo in the far reaches of my memory banks.

I am now committed to surgically removing all drama and negativity from my life, and in case there are any delayed reactions from my shooting; like post-traumatic stress, or anything like that, I took a two-day course, learning all about transcendental meditation and it seems to be working wonders for me; it keeps me calm, my thoughts are less muddled, and I feel like I have more energy. The TM instructor, Angela, gifted me with my own sacred mantra, and it will stay with me forever.

I make my way down the stairs and into the living room. Mum is watching one of her shitey TV programmes, she stands up as soon as she sees me, gives me a big hug and tells me, "I am going to miss you son." I hug her back and reassure her, "I'll miss you too, Ma. Where is Dad?" "Oh, playing Golf as usual." I bet you, that with the money I gave my parents, Dad has gone tonto and bought a brand new range of golf clubs, sneaky old dog that he is. I'll find the right time over the next day or so to say farewell to Dad, I need to make sure that I get all my goodbyes out of the way – after word of me getting shot reached the boys, they got in touch again. It was awkward, it started with a few text messages coming and going, then a couple of calls, but the long and short of it is, that I am flying out to meet them, in Australia no less. I can't wait, I feel as light as a feather.

Mum offers me a cup of tea, "no thanks, Ma. I think that I'll go and stretch my legs. I won't be long." I slip my shoes on and make my way outside, looking up towards the hill, what I see has me smiling like a Cheshire cat – it's him, it's Walter, sat alone on the bench. For the first time, I have seen him before he has had the chance to sneak up on me. I will miss Walter, but I won't miss him startling the living shit out of me.

As I approach Walter, he stands up, taller than I remember him being, and it's only been a few weeks since I saw him last, but without a word spoken, he grabs me in an almighty embrace. Eventually, he says into my ear, "it's good to see you son." My head buried in his chest, I acknowledge him by giving him a couple of pats on the back. Walter lets me go, and we both take a seat. This is ample opportunity to say farewell. "Walter, my friends and I have patched things up, and I have decided to join them in Australia." Walter, nodding in approval, "that's great news, Joe."

I can't let this opportunity slip through my fingers, I need to let him know just how much he helped me and what his companionship means to me, so much so, that I am not sure that I will be able to fully articulate what I want to say. "Walter, I just have to thank you for.." Immediately, Walter raises his hand to gesture that I should stop right there. "There is no need to thank me for anything Joe my boy. I am just glad that you are still here and that you had the opportunity to patch things up with your pals and you are flying out to meet them. Besides, I am going on a trip myself; my son is home for a visit, and we have decided to finally make the trip over the pond and tag along on his return flight, to see Stewart's home. Maybe spend a few weeks out there, who knows."

Just then, a car pulls up at the bottom of the hill, right next to my house. A man steps out and yells towards us, "hey Dad. You ready?" Walter smiles as he springs to his feet, "that's Stewart there. Come on, let me introduce you to him."

As we make our way down the path, along the hill, Stewart walks closer towards us, before introducing himself. "You must be Joe, right? I have heard a lot about you kid." As I shake his hand, I cannot help but notice just how much he looks like a younger version of Walter. But I have barely had the chance to geek out over their resemblance when I hear "Hello son", coming from the back of the car. I move closer, Walter informs me, "Joe, this is my wife, Rose." The rear passenger window rolled all the way down, and there looking out at me is an old lady with the most piercing blue eyes. "So, you're the young fella that my Walter has been fretting about. Well, you look as fit as a fiddle now. I mean, some young floozy causing such a stooshy. Oh well, hell knock it into her, I say", Rose declares, before bursting out laughing. Quickly composing herself, Rose tells me, "it was nice to meet you. However, we must be going", as she slowly winds the window back up. Stewart checks his watch, "Dad, Mom's right." Stewart makes his way back into the car, Walter offers me his hand, "Joe, when you get back from your travels, we'll meet on that hill for a blether, and we can talk about our trips." I shake Walter's hand, "Walter, I will never forget you." Walter releases his hand and pats me on the side of the arm, "I know you won't, Joe. I know you won't." Walter pops his cap on, gives me a sly grin, turns and gets into the car.

Stewart makes a three-point-turn, getting the car into position. Once facing the right direction, the car creeps forward, all three of them give me a wave, before the car speeds up, and then they're gone. As I watch their car fade into the distance, I feel this pang in my heart; I hope that this is not the last time that I get to see Walter. I bow my head for a moment, goodbyes are brutal.

I go back inside, in the hall I can hear the start of the ad break on the TV. Mum shouts through to me, once again asking, "putting the kettle on, love, if you fancy a cuppa now?" I make my way through to the kitchen, "yeah, sure, thanks Ma. Milk, no sugar please." Just then, Mum remembers something, "oh, before you get too comfy, Dad has asked if you could move his old golf bag out of the dining room and put it in the garage." Haha, I knew the first thing he'd do with the money I gave him was upgrade his golf regalia.

I make my way out to the garage. Placing the golf bag down in the far corner, I notice that the garage is still pretty clean since I gave it a right good clear-out in preparation for my book club, that fell on its arse. "Hello Joe." I would know that voice anywhere, I turn around, it's Apollina, and she is standing on the exact same spot that I saw her the first time we met. "I saw what happened to you, on the news. It is good to see you well. Would you like to come and walk with me?"

We make our way out of my street, we walk and walk, as we have a right good natter; eventually Apollina asks how I am feeling, and she doesn't react much when I tell her, that once I have tied up a couple of loose ends, I am leaving and I don't know when I will come back. Apollina informs me, "I too have to go. My mother is sick, and I don't know quite how serious it is yet. I have spoken to the university, and I will just need to take things as they come." I am not really sure what to say. "I am sorry to hear that. I hope that your Mum gets better soon, and you get to stay", secretly, and selfishly, hoping that she is still around when I return from Oz.

Apollina takes my hands, "Joe, when we met in the coffee shop, and you told me all of those things, at first it was disturbing to me. But then, I realised that I respected your openness, your vulnerability. We may never see each other, ever again. Tonight, would you like to stay with me; a fond farewell, so to speak." Oh my,

I'm bursting out my breeks. "Yes. Oh God, yes. Yes, that sounds, just lovely." How lucky am I? And I shaved my arse and pubic sector this morning – talk about good timing.

"YOU!" What the? "DIRTY WEE BASTARD!!!" It's the dog walker. Fuck it, I'm off.

Running as fast as I can, running like an absolute maniac – the dog walker, and his dog, once more chasing me in hot pursuit, and again, the adrenaline tearing through me, and despite all of this, I find the clarity of thought, "that's right, that's right. Get to sleep with Apollina? Of course not. Don't be stupid-stupid."

I turn my head for a moment, I am so far away from Apollina, I can barely make her out; her arms out stretched, as if to say "WHAT. THE. FUCK?" I have quite literally left her for dust.

Running, running, I'm in better shape than the last time this mental old bastard chased me. I am confident that I will be able to outrun him more quickly this time. However, I can hear sirens, I hope they're not for me. I may have some candy in the bank, but money won't save me from the Police or this guy battering my head in with his dog lead. What's to say that he won't make a point of telling Apollina about that night of the "drop-off", when he busted me fly-tipping, with my piece hanging out? How would I explain that to her? Anyways, I strongly suspect that her being witness to me being suddenly, and angrily, chased by a middle-aged man, is the nail in the coffin of any prospects, of what looked like a sure-fire guaranteed night of wild freaky jungle love action.

Running, running. I'm off to Australia in a matter of days – I suspect that there aren't any dog walkers over there who think that I am a pervert, all I have to worry about is the seventeen million different species of deadly creatures that they have. I fucking hate spiders.

32319548R00141

Printed in Poland
by Amazon Fulfillment
Poland Sp. z o.o., Wrocław